sight

Sol Smith

1

sol smith

sight

Things that are done, it is needless to speak about...things that are past, it is needless to blame.

-Confucius

chapter 1

sol smith

Tydomin White

Nov. 16, 2006

He's in here again. Derek. He's been in the store the last three or four nights in a row. The first time he came in, I recognized him. I knew that we were going to date. It wasn't a mystery. But for whatever reason, he's having really hard time finding his way over to talk to me. He watches me from the corners of his eyes the whole time he waltzes around the small bookstore. I can see him tracking me around and through the shelves, over the pages of books that are selected just to impress me as far as I can tell. He bought something the first day, but ever since, he's been hesitant. Tonight, I know, he'll say goodbye to me, over his shoulder as he's leaving. Tomorrow night, he'll buy a couple more books. But again, he won't ask me out. He won't ask me my name.

    I knew he'd come in, so I put on my cutest skirt. I

feel like if I can just push this thing along—whatever his attraction to me is—I can move forward and find out what this whole damn thing, find out what it's about. So on the nights when he comes, I'm sure to turn on his favorite music. He's probably the only person I will ever meet who loves 15th Century classical music so much. He'll end up majoring in it in college, and I think that's a brave thing. Who majors in something that they know—like *know* without a single doubt—will not pay the bills in the end? Musicians. I guess I have a thing for them, and maybe that's why we end up going out. I hope I don't look like a little doe in the headlights to every guy who can put a minor chord together. God, why can't I be more confident about this kind of thing.

But still, even with the stage set, with the lights low, with the music he loves surrounding him, with my flowing brown-earth peasant skirt, my hair in a half-ponytail, practically screaming "hey ren-fair music guy! Look at me!" he doesn't come up and ask me out. He must find me attractive if we're going to date. I just don't get him. I just don't get this situation, I guess.

It's no wonder that a couple nights from now, on my night off, I'm going to wait for him at his table at the coffee shop across the way, under Abigail's judgmental eyes. He'll be surprised, or at least act the part. And I will entertain him by letting him introduce himself to me, though I really feel like I know him already and have for about two years now. I've been painting pictures of him while practicing my vision.

After I finished the first picture that I painted of him, I sat and studied it. I knew it was someone that I was going to date, have some kind of serious relationship with. But I couldn't really understand why. I didn't find him altogether attractive, but not totally unappealing. I hadn't even met Erica or Vic yet, so his relationship to them really meant nothing to me. Then I moved down to the valley. And then I saw him for the first time, very briefly, at one of Abigail's concerts down near Mission Square. I looked at him there, and he was entirely unaware of me, and again I wondered what it was I was going to see in him; quiet and reserve weren't exactly the qualities I was looking for in a guy, and they weren't anything like what everyone liked about Vic.

He represents the last stage of my life before I leave this town. Everything that I've worked for comes to fruition just a week or so after we break up. My art sells, I move to San Francisco, and I leave all of this behind me. This strange weaving of characters that I've met here in Ashlan—Vic, Derek, Abigail, and Martin, that telepath who I will see again before too long—I finally leave them all behind. I don't know exactly how dating Derek works into this, but I'm anxious to get it over with; I've been waiting too long for this success to come, working too hard on my art, staying up night after night since I was little just to have my work displayed in the museum up there. One last hurdle that springs me out of this bookstore, out of this town, and away from the dreadful prospect of whoring my visions for a living, but embracing my unique perspective as an artist. And this short relationship is somehow the last step.

But I have to own up to it; I *know* that he is somehow significant. I know we don't date that long, but that he must end up meaning something to me. This is really hard to see. I start talking to him about things, about the way that time is for me. He's the first person I've seen since moving to Ashlan that I actually end up talking about my vantage of the world—not in warning him of the future and not informing him about his past—but in some way of sympathy, of sharing my burden. That must mean something, right? Opening up to some *normal* person about it? I mean, Vic found out, and that didn't exactly end well.

I tell him about how I see the world, opened up like a disjointed book, forwards and backwards. Sometimes I see future events dictate the past—like I must go through a moment now because of what has already happened later and how it needs this moment to come into existence (the day the curator wanders into this bookstore, for example, and admires my work seems to bring my relationship with Derek into being weeks before; something that would make very little sense to so many people). Sometimes, I tell him, I see how moments from the past come forward and haunt us, how many people are still stuck in that moment in every way but the physical, and how easy it is be lost in the past. And I hold back from telling him all that stuff about his brother, how he had known and he had...well, Vic made his decision.

At first, I didn't actually see me talking to him about this; it was just a little too far off for me to see the time. But, I saw, I *would* see myself talking to him about this. I was taught to use these visions within visions to see further and further, but the messages still seem very muddled to me, and echo of an echo coming from over the horizon. But now I see, very clearly, that I say to him, "You have to understand what the world is like for me, Derek. I couldn't have known that we would be in love."

Love? I can't imagine looking at him and thinking that I will someday think I'm in love with him. He seems childish, juvenile, despite what everyone says about him being smart or whatever. I imagine that it's something I say to let him down easy; a little white lie to make him feel better about whatever it was that passes between us. Poor kid.

And now, as he wanders the store, I have to ask myself again. He's an admirer, and he's kind of cute. Though younger than the other boys I've dated, he's still older than me. But he won't even talk to me unless he's armed with an impressive book of some kind. And it's going to take me making the first move just to find out what it is that I am going to find intriguing about him.

Now his brother, that was a different story. Good looking was just the beginning of him. Maybe it's the shadow of his brother that he lives under that makes him so timid. I just keep thinking, he's Vic's brother for god's sake. I still feel guilty about what happened to Vic and I just can't believe that his little brother has somehow become attracted to me. It feels dishonest not to tell him, but it's too complex.

And maybe that's why we're drawn to each other. Both of us have had out lives decided by a car accident. Like the plagues of our day, car accidents can take anyone without discrimination. We're both wounded by loss. Maybe we're pulled together by the vacancies in our lives. Maybe we'll try and fill the void for each other.

I sigh, head heavy in my hand, elbow resting on the top of the register. I don't want us to be pathetic together. I don't want us to give pity to each other. Maybe there's more. Damn. I'm going to have to make a move and try and crack this egg. Like I've known I'm going to.

I can hardly muster the energy to smile at him when he says "good-bye" to me over his shoulder. Poor boy.

Martin Oaks

October 16th, 1991

The Spirit has finally found me. Momma has been
wishing and praying to God and his baby for as long as I
can remember. She tells me to pray that The Spirit will
talk, but I could never hear God answer. He whispers
to Momma's heart, so that only she and her heart can
hear, and she doesn't mind that God's baby cries,
because all babies do cry most of the time, right? And
Momma, I'm sure, can hear it in her heart and it
doesn't make her mad. It made her mad when my
baby brother cried a lot, but then again, he's not God's
baby, is he? He's the demon seed, she says.

Turns out, God's baby died too.

I'm sitting down for breakfast. Momma sets a blue

bowl full of oatmeal on the kitchen table right in front of me. The spoon is a little too big for me, but it's all she has clean, goddamn it, so I'd better use it. The scooper part of the spoon is the size of my hand and a mouthful of oatmeal from this spoon would probably drown me. So I'd better be careful. We can't have two drown babies, now can we?

I blow in the oatmeal. I watch the smoke white-hot curl in the air. There must be fire in my oatmeal, because there's smoke and where there's smoke there has got to be. I blow and blow like it is a birthday cake instead of just oatmeal. I sing the birthday song in my head and blow on the oatmeal. I sing the birthday song moving my mouth and the words and I blow out the oatmeal. I pretend to put four candles in the oatmeal, the chocolate oatmeal with chocolate icing. A match flashes from my Uncle Rob's thumb and he lights the candles. The party hat string is too tight on my chin, but the hat is covered with stars, blue and yellow, and the Power Rangers plates are all passed around.

Everyone is singing. They sing so loud and happy and even my baby brother Max is there wide-bright eyes so shining with everyone singing. We sing and I sing out loud my birthday song. I blow out the candles and clap my hands loud.

Wham.

Momma claps my head. I've been lost in day dreaming again and can't I just shut up to eat my goddamn oatmeal?

I stare at the oatmeal. At the spoon. And this is when The Spirit finally finds me. He takes that oatmeal smoke, that birthday candle smoke, and breathes it deep into my head. It fills my eyes, watching two bowls of oatmeal and two spoons criss and cross each other, over and out of each other, around and into each other. The smoke gets thick and now I hear it. Momma's voice. But she's not talking her voice is in the smoke.

"God, my God," she is saying. "Why God, Why?"

She sits down. Wringing my hands then twisting my hair with one finger. I can see the back of my head from where Momma is sitting. She opens her mouth and together we say, "Eat your damn oatmeal." And she jumps from the startle of me saying the same words from inside my head.

The Spirit stops his whispering, surprised too, I guess, and I'm looking at the just one bowl of oatmeal and just one big spoon.

Momma steps closer to me, but I don't turn around. "How did you know what I was going to say?"

"I think The Spirit has found me, Momma. He's whispering things in my heart."

16

She comes from behind me and looks in my eyes. Her eyes are red and bloody. "Good," she says real quiet. "Good. Now you pray, Martin. You pray for forgiveness for those words. And you pray for my forgiveness too, you hear me young man?"

Her robe flies out behind her as she storms out of the kitchen and I hear her footsteps going up the stairs.

"Spirit," I say. "Spirit, you tell God that I'm sorry." And my eyes go crossed again, looking again at two spoons and two tables out in front of me. And The Spirit breathes the deep smoke into my head again.

I'm busy making Momma's footsteps again. I brush my long hair back over my shoulders. I should get it cut soon, for Christ sake. I push open Momma's bedroom door and step lightly now not to bang the floor above the kitchen with too much noise because he'd better finish his fucking oatmeal.

Red, yellow, and two white pills. I swallow them so easy with Momma's mouth, not like when she tries to make me swallow pills and I need them crushed up in ice cream. I look in the mirror. Momma's face is drooping with red eyes and I just look like shit from getting no sleep. The splash of water doesn't help how I look and we start to cry. A choke feeling, like the time

I tripped when eating a lifesaver, starts in Momma's throat. Then we burst hard into the sobbing with the tears down her cheeks that I always see her doing in her room.

She turns and I see the bathtub. I want to look away. The curtain is closed over the tub and I don't want to watch while Momma's hand lifts up and pulls it away. No, please God it didn't happen. Our arm throws the curtain back and her knees hit hard on the ground and my regular ears downstairs hear the sound while I feel it on Momma's legs.

Max looks blue and white and puffy under the water. What the hell am I going to do? Momma asks. Dear God take this back wash our sins! Dear God strike me down and bring this child back, this lamb, dear God.

I hear a bang when Momma hits the floor and suddenly I'm looking at my oatmeal again. I take a bite and it's not too hot any more. For some reason, even though it's morning, the room looks a little dark and it's hard to see the table. Thing are blurry around me.

Whisper, Spirit, but show me something happy.

Red Scabergrade

Dec. 21, 1997

It's unfortunate that Alan is coming today. There's still so much to be done to get ready for the girl. I've begun compartmentalizing my dates based on events, which I never used to do when I was younger. It worries me. Instead of the chaos that I used to see when I was a child, I see perfect, crystalline organization. That's not really any more real than the visions of chaos.

I didn't notice, really, until yesterday that my package from Eric is getting here the same day that Alan is coming. He's coming unannounced, of course, which gives me a fine excuse to be as busy as I am. I can't think of the last time that I had a client come unannounced. But he will pay well enough for me to bow out of working for quite some time. That will be helpful.

I drive my truck back up the drive now, with a package in the passenger seat. Eric sent it yesterday and it got to my PO box today. He called this morning to see that it got there safely, and that I should know that it was even sent, but I was gone to pick it up when the phone rang. I changed the outgoing message on my answering machine to say, "Thanks, Eric. I'll call you when I get a chance to go through everything."

That should irritate him.

I park my truck in the garage and walk around to the front of the house. From the porch, I can see the San Joaquin valley spread out below me, the fog just lifting off the streets. The morning is quiet and the air is thin and crisp. Autumn is passing into winter. Winter of 1997. It's here. The anticipation over the last seven years has nearly killed me.

In this same week, I will meet someone who would like to kill me and the one person who may end up giving my life some kind of meaning.

I open the door and walk through the foyer. I run my hand along my piano, regretting that there just aren't enough moments to play right now. I turn to my office and sit in the leather seat, spilling the contents of the package out on the desk before me.

A driver's license. A birth certificate, weathered and worn. A resume. Four years of tax records. A passport, with stamps of 6 countries. Pay stubs from the last year and a half. My picture, but not my history. All purchased for the price of one lottery ticket.

I take out the driver's license. My picture, my address. But the name printed on it is not quite mine. As a matter of fact, as far as aliases go, this one is too comical. Red White.

I pick up the phone. I dial a number in Langley.

"Red," the voice says.

"Did you have to make the name so impractical?"

He chuckles a little. "I did what I thought was best."

"And your best includes this name that sounds like two-thirds of a July Fourth party?"

He laughs out loud now, but hardly at my joke. "I told you, Red, it's the simplest way. CPS is going to look at the last name and see that they match. You're a paternal relative and that's the most straight-forward way to go about it, the least possible questions. I asked my friend in the bureau, he's a stickler for paperwork like this."

"You could have changed the first name."

We don't know how much the girl knows about

you. She could call you Red right there in front of everyone and you're going to have to backpedal to make up some kind of a nickname story. You've worked in the agency long enough to know that's not a cool plan."

I sigh. "The records?"

"All straight."

"Other relatives?"

"Nope. Practically none."

"What," I growl, "do you mean by 'practically'?"

"The grandparents are dead, except for one in an Alzheimer's ward in Modesto. There's a second cousin in Oregon on the mother's side that appears to have no contact with them. That's all I can find, and believe me, we've been thorough. So as long as you're right about the, you know, tragedy, I have to congratulate you."

"On what?"

"C'mon, Red; your going to be a father!"

"That's not the point."

"Isn't it?"

He's brash, Eric. I give him room to make all the fun he wants. He started at the agency just a couple years before I left. He's a desk jockey with every connection in the universe. He's been working on this project for a little over a year, trying to sneak most of it in on company time, I imagine.

We agreed about payment before hand. It had to be a slow week, the jackpot not so high as to bring a lot of attention. He had to accept the cash-value. And it had to be a week when there were multiple winners. That last stipulation had him sore for a while, but he got over it. His modest take in the end was almost three million dollars.

He's been giddy every time I've talked to him in the last couple weeks.

"How are things at the company?"

"Same ol'. I mean, there's a new head of the department."

"I know."

"I'll bet. And I'll bet you know about the changes she wants to make."

"Will make," I corrected. "And you plan to stay on despite your windfall?"

"Yeah, yeah. I just can't seem to shake this job. It's too exciting just to walk away."

I nod my head at the phone. "Some people find it very exhilarating."

"You did, didn't you?"

I think about the answer to this for a second. "For a time. But exploitation is exploitation, no matter how exhilarating, Eric."

"You peripherals are all the same," Eric says. "You see the big picture so well, you can't just indulge in the moment. Every job is exploitation."

"You wouldn't use a handicapped person for their handicap."

"Sure, Red, you don't. But what handicap is as useful as seeing the future?"

"That's not the point. The point is that it's not a talent, it's not a skill, it's not something to be proud of. There is no honor in doing it for a living. When a seer works for someone that way, it's nothing less than a prostitution. You use a skill, something you've worked on for many years. Projectors may have different levels of talent, but remote viewing can be taught, you can be trained. This is something I was born with; there's no creativity to it, there's no beauty to be found in it. I sell myself when I use this for profit, Eric. I may as well just win a lottery myself. I may as well rook people out of their money for a living like so many of us do."

"Like you're going to do with this guy."

"A means to an end, Eric. It all adds up to a chance for this poor orphan to not sell her soul. To discover the possibilities of using this handicap as a form of expression. You understand all of this."

"Sure," Eric says. "I understand, Daddy Warbucks."

I hear a car coming up the gravel drive, as I had

expected. "He's here, Eric."

"Who?"

"The next guy I'm going to rook out of money. My next trick. I'll have to talk to you later."

"Whatever you say, Red. Take care of yourself."

"I'll call you if I have anymore questions."

Abigail Winters

Dec. 21, 1997

Mom is taking me and Vic to the movies. We're going to see *Titanic* because we're practically the only kids in the 5th grade that didn't go see it on opening day. We barely ever go to the movies unless they're in the discount theater. It's easier to do it that way, without the crowds and it's the closest one to our house. But this is different. Even my mom has heard too much about it to not go right away.

Dad is staying at home to get more grading done. Midterms. Seems like if he's not on vacation for summer or Christmas, it's always midterms or finals and he gets so busy I never see him. I think it bothers mom to never see him, too.

Mom has been having bad headaches lately. On Monday she's going to have an MRI, where they look into her head and find out if it's a tumor or not. Dad and I know that it's nothing, and we keep telling her so. She has been doing some kind of ritual at night in the backyard, trying to get rid of them, but that hasn't worked either. I told her that I'm sorry her head hurts, but I don't want her to embarrass me by complaining about it all night in front of Vic. She's doing a good job, because I can see her hands tighten around the steering wheel of our Volvo. She closes her eyes tight and I can tell that her head is hurting pretty bad all of a sudden.

The light from the traffic lights paints her squinting face green, but she doesn't move.

"It's green, Mom," I say.

"I know, honey." I can hear the pain hidden in her voice. The car behind us honks. Vic looks at me. I shrug.

The car behind us swings around us to just go on ahead through the intersection. Oh my God, it's embarrassing.

"You okay, Mom?"

She turns with a half-smile to look at me sitting in the back seat. While she's smiling at me, she opens her mouth to say something, but never gets it out because the little white car that drove around us is hit by a truck coming the other way.

It's sudden. Like one second it's not there, then there's this sound. The sound is horrible and loud, deafening, when the two cars bounce away from each other. I don't ever see the hit, really, just the bouncing apart.

Panic paints my mom's face. Vic says, "Should we help them?"

Mom turns around to talk, and that's when the whole thing blows. Our side windows shatter and the little white car is on fire. It's dark outside but now it's like daytime, the fire is so bright. Even in the car behind the cracked windshield, we can feel the heat from the fire.

Mom puts the car in reverse, and we back up into a parking lot.

"We have to help," Vic says.

"You two need to be safe," Mom says.

Two older boys hop out of the truck and run off on foot, when they see what they did to the smaller car. Stupid.

Mom gets out of the car after telling us to sit still. She inches towards the wreck, but either the heat or her headache holds her back. She yells when she sees a hand hit the window from the driver's side.

Someone tries kicking in the window, but it gets too hot for him and he backs off. I look at our windows, shattered to pieces, and wonder what cruel trick made theirs stay together. "It's a much newer car," Vic says. "The safety glass has gotten much better."

Safety glass. Shame.

The fire department gets here pretty quickly. Between the light from the fire and the flashing of the sirens, I have a hard time seeing everything. I try to shield my eyes, but I have to keep watching.

Mom gets back in the car with tears running down her cheeks. "It looks like a woman and a man," she says.

"They'll save them, right?" I ask.

She shakes her head, saying she doesn't know. But we can all see it's probably too late.

Vic, eyes wide, says, "What a horrible way to die." He says what we're all thinking.

Derek Neely

December 16, 2006

There's a dream that I always have where I'm lying on my back, looking at the stars. The stars are impossibly bright and textured, like patches of wildflowers on the side of a highway. I can see them moving, rotating, changing trajectories. Dust blows off of them, like so much pollen.

"It was in the stars, man," I hear a voice saying.

I turn and it's my brother, Vic. I'm his age now, which is as strange as my view of the stars.

"It's not your fault, you know?"

I tell him that I don't care if it was my fault or not. The fact that he's not here is enough for me to be pretty bent out of shape.

"It doesn't matter, bro," he says, coolly. "You remember the funeral? All those people talking about God and about the eternal? Well, what stood out to you the most?"

I don't want to tell him what it was. I don't want to sound so mundane.

"I know, bro," he says. "Astroturf and lawn chairs. You guys are all sitting around a big-ass hole in the ground on folding chairs, right? Dinky little plastic folding chairs. And there's that pile of dirt covered with a sloppy patch of Astroturf. And people are barking around about God. Some holy scene, right?"

His funeral is something that I still see when I shut my eyes tightly. The whole thing was so contrived— just some regular day without anything special going on when we put him in the ground. It seemed so terribly meaningless.

"Let me tell you about God, bro. I've met him. And the whole thing is silly. He's just some kid, like us. He wanted to impress people—never mind you who—he was a showoff kid who made this whole *world* thing, and this whole *love* thing, and everyone gets a kick watching what's going on down here, everyone praises the little prodigy that made the fancy little trinket.

"The thing is, it's out of his control. He looks down on us now and doesn't know what to do. I don't know if He's gotten kind of attached, or if He's embarrassed that He can't control everything, or what. But He's at a loss all of a sudden. It's kind of funny, you know? Like we're all looking to Him for guidance, and He just wishes He thought twice."

"That sounds awful cynical," I say to him.

31

"Yeah. I guess that's what I see because I find it so reassuring. Like my life makes sense because nothing makes sense anyway, right? You'll see something greater, I'm sure. You'll see things like these stars, right?"

I look up at the stars again. Their movements are so precise and magical; exact and beautiful. It's a ballet of thoughtful and accurate *meaning*. "It's all so wonderful," I tell him. "There's so much purpose to it."

"That was always the difference between us, bro," he says. "But there's enough truth for both of us, right?"

I wake up from this dream with his voice still ringing in my ears. I wonder what I would have done that day, if only I could have read the meaning in the stars, the balance of events, and could have saved his life.

And I wonder if there's something in the stars now that could point *her* to me.

chapter 2

sol smith

Tydomin White

Dec. 20th, 1997

I use *timberwolf* for most of the body of the car. It was white, but the paint burns away so quickly and the aluminum won't char away for a while longer. Only the very back where the explosion happens do I touch with black. The flames are a complex mixture. The top layer, barely a wisp, is *wild strawberry*. Directly under it is *violet red* then *red* for a good portion of the body of the flames. There's a stripe of *red-orange* leading into *orange,* and into *melon* before getting into the yellows at the center. As for the yellows, it's a quick *dandelion* before getting into *yellow.*

    I look at the 64-pack of crayons that Dad gave me and I wonder if there's a way I can make this fire look brighter on the page. In the end, the flames that look like a sunset are still flat. There's no brightness to it. There's no body. I know that when this happens, Mom and Dad will feel the heat that my crayons just can't draw. That center yellow spot will be too bright to look at.

I sharpen the black crayon in the sharpener and peel back the paper. The smoke is dark *black* with a shapely outer edge of *gunmetal gray*. It billows in the middle and dies off on the outside. I need the crayon sharp to lightly define the sections.

The bushes and trees in the background are hard to see. They're half hidden in shadow, but illuminated with a mixture of light from the fire and flashes from the police car that is near by. In the end I settle on *forest green* as a base, with light flashes of *melon* and *midnight blue*.

The front tire is bent in, folded under the rest of the car. The hood is pushed back like when Mom pushes back a cuticle. The other car with the teenaged boys bounced off the page, but you can still see the bumper on the edge of the picture.

I can't color the sound of the bouncing, but it plays in my head over and over as I draw. I usually think of metal as solid and hard. But it sounds like folding and crumpling, like a piece of paper being thrown away turned up a thousand times. And when the other car bounces off, there is a rubber dragged over pavement sound and an almost funny spring sound, if it weren't so loud and scary.

The smell isn't like the fire we have in our fireplace tonight. Not like our marshmallow fire that we had when we went camping last summer. That fire was put out by the rain and the smell was wonderful like musky flowers. Mom was mad at me when it rained. She was mad because I told her it would rain and that we should go another weekend and she didn't want it to happen. She never wants anything I tell her to happen. She always gets mad. So I try to keep things to myself as much as I can.

She even got mad when I saved her plate. She was going to drop it, so I put a pillow on the ground where it would fall. She was so upset, crying, that I got the dish and threw it on the floor. She wanted to wipe the smile off my face. I just didn't know—did she want the plate or not? Why would saving it make her cry and breaking it make her mad?

I'm almost finished with the picture when I decide to stop. Mom and Dad have been giving my pictures to Dr. Torrance ever since they bought me the new paper and crayons. I told them I wanted colored pencils or charcoals, but they said that 7 year olds should use crayons, even if they are advanced learners.

Every Monday and Thursday we stop our classes in the living room and talk to Dr. Torrance. He talks all afternoon about my pictures and why I draw them and why I think they're real. He wants to find the source of my detachment, too.

I spent a long time looking at Dr. Torrance during our last meeting. I saw where he grew up. His mom in her suit slipped in and out of their apartment. His nanny lived in the room next to his and when he'd have a bad dream, he'd sneak into her bed. Before the sun rose, she would put him back in his room and they'd whisper about it over breakfast if his mom was there.

When they left San Francisco, he cried. They moved here to Ashlan and his mom got to spend more time with him. He was sour, she would say, because he missed the city and the sounds. But really, he never told her, he missed his nanny. When he came home from school, it was his mom that picked him up and then sat at the table pouring over papers. When he had a bad dream, he stayed in his bed by himself and cried into his pillow, pretending his nanny was there.

I take the picture of the car accident and fold it as many times as I can—five times—and put it under my bed. I pull out a new piece of paper and look over my shoulder. Mom is watching TV, all alone with herself. She didn't see the picture and she didn't see the new paper I brought out. On the new paper, I start to draw Dr. Torrance's nanny. Maybe he will find this interesting. I peel off the papers from the colors I will use. I use the sides of crayons, long wide strokes, since I want to show how Dr. Torrance *felt* about his nanny.

Mom is on "All My Children," I can tell. So I only have an hour or so for the picture. Then Dr. Torrance will be here. I hurry.

Martin Oaks

October 20, 1991

Momma and I are sitting in church. On our knees.
We're way up front with our knees on a wooden step
made for knees. Church service is over, but we're here
anyway because we're some of God's very favorites.
We stay after every service lately.

The Spirit talks to me all the time now. He breaths
the smoke into me and I see all kinds of different
things. Right now, I look up at God, hanging on the
wall, all naked and sad. I can't see it very well at all,
just what's in the middle is all I can see anymore.
Everything around God's face is dark shapes all running
together like finger paints. But if I say a real quick
prayer to The Spirit, I can see God through Momma's
eyes and it's all better and clear.

I can hear Momma talking, too. Her lips are moving fast with "Mary full of lace," but inside her head, she's still thinking over and over about yesterday.

We went outside in the backyard to do some really fun yard stuff. I bumped into the side of the door on the way out, then fell down the step. I couldn't see anything very well outside, so The Spirit showed me what I looked like on the ground through Momma's eyes so I could see myself stand up and come over to help Momma. I made faces at her then like in a mirror and laughed. I looked really funny.

"You stop that," Momma yelled. "We're here for very serious work."

She took a long shovel and gave me a spade. We got to dig the biggest hole I've ever seen right there in the yard. I kept watching myself dig through Momma's eyes. It was more fun.

After we had a big hole, she told me how I got to help dig because this was also my fault that Max died. That if she didn't have me there, she would have taken care of Max, rest his soul. We put his little baby body in the ground, all blue and white, and covered him up. We both cried so loud when it was done.

"What the hell have I done?" she was thinking. "Oh God, forgive us, what in the name of God have I done?"

We walked inside and she wouldn't make me a tuna sandwich. It was getting too late to have a goddamn tuna sandwich, but I was tired and hungry. We worked so hard and so long and all I wanted was a tuna sandwich. "Why not Momma?" I asked. "What in the name of God have I done? Oh God, forgive us, what the hell have I done?"

She made me the sandwich after that. I told her it was a good sandwich and that I thought that God would forgive her, rest her soul and rest Max's soul, because the sandwich was so good.

Now she's looking up at God and thinking about it over and over. I don't hear God in her head, not at all, so I know that God is not talking to her, even though she keeps on and on talking to God. I keep up inside The Spirit's smoke so I can stay inside Momma's head and stay looking at God through her eyes. He's so sad. Even with his crown, God is sad. I think that maybe he knows how bad Momma feels about Max, and that's what's making him sad, even though Max is with Him now, he doesn't want Momma to be sad.

Momma shuts her eyes tight.

I shut my eyes tight.

We see the day that Max wouldn't stop crying. The day after my birthday. We see how Momma shook and shook him and he won't stop crying. Momma is screaming at him and Little-Max-God-Rest-His-Soul screams back with his eyes closed. I tell Max to stop crying, too, but in my head where no one can hear it because I don't want Momma to be mad anymore.

Then Momma is pushing the baby down under water and thank god he finally shut up, the demon. His fucking father will hear about this in jail and fuck him for acting like he cares in the first place. I can feel the smile stretch across Momma's face when Max stops kicking.

Now she tries to pull him out and he's not crying or kicking. Now Momma is right next to me in the church and she opens her eyes and we see God up on the wall, sadder than ever. We sob together. I hear her asking Hail Mary Full of Lace about open gates for the young deceased. Blessed is the fruit of her loom, Jesus, Mother of God pray for the sinners now at the hour of death amen. She says it too fast and over and over.

I leave Momma and am back in my head, looking up at God. I can't see him very much at all now. Just shapes and lights. I think about Mary, and how she uses her lace to make fruit from her looms that can save people. I hope that we don't die in an hour, like the people Momma is talking about.

In the car, I am sitting in my booster seat. I close

my eyes and because I get a little sick looking at the dark blurry shapes passing by the window.

"Why are you so quiet?" Momma asks. She wipes away all her tears.

"I don't want to cry anymore," I tell her.

"Why not? We are very sad, Martin. It's okay to cry when you are sad."

"Oh." I say. I think about God and how he cries. I think about Max and how much he cried. "I don't want to cry too much. I don't want you to push me in the bath."

Now she's crying again. I don't want to leave my head and I ask The Spirit not to talk to me right now. I don't like the things Momma thinks.

Red Scabergrade

December 21, 1997

Alan is exactly the kind of man you'd expect an assassin to be. Clean cut, quiet, and constantly on guard. He is balding, but cuts his hair low. His nose sticks out in front of him like a knife coming down from his forehead. I can see him assessing the house as he comes in, watching for exits, weapons, and cover. His hands are folded in front of him and he strolls as if he is walking down the halls of a museum. I get the feeling that after he walks through a group of people, none of them agree on his description later.

"This is an impressive home, Mr. Scabergrade."

"Thank you," I say. "If I might ask, how did you presume to come all the way up here without an appointment?"

"Mr. Scabergrade, your reputation precedes you. If you are as good as everyone says you are, then you certainly expected me." He smiles wryly, as if he had just caught me in something.

sol smith

"Indeed I did," I say. "And I have a cup of red tea waiting for you in my office. But there is still a courtesy in arranging a meeting."

"I'm sorry. I'll know better in the future."

I motion for him to follow me and together we walk through the living room. After scanning the room in its entirety, he looks for a long while out the back window. The windows are two stories tall and provide a wonderful view of the surrounding forest covered in snow.

"So," I say as we enter my office. "Who was it that referred you?"

"Of course I've heard of you many times, Mr. Scabergrade."

"Is that so?"

"I worked for the CIA and had friends in the peripheral department. You are a legend there."

"Yes, a legend of uncooperativeness."

He nods his head. "There is that. I've heard plenty about your problems with the program. But everyone says that you never miss anything."

"That may be so, but how did you find me?"

"You are not so hard a man to find, Mr. Scabergrade. Ann Diamond was a client of yours. She pointed me in this direction."

Ann was a second-rate real estate baron from

46

Ashlan. I had advised her years before to buy up a lot of useless fig orchards in an area neighboring Ashlan. She was able to sell it to developers for twenty times the cost just two years later. The growth in that area was unprecedented, and though her land ended up being over priced, it was fully necessary for the other real estate ventures in the area. It was a simple killing.

"Are you into real estate, Mr. Saunders?"

"I am. Actually, insurance. But real estate as well."

"How do you propose that I help you?"

He smiles and starts reaching for his brief case. "Would you like to see everything I have worked up?"

"I can almost assure you that I do not want to see it," I say. "I rarely understand the full plans of my clients, and it generally works better that way. You pay for information, not for a partner."

He nods his head. "Good. Very good."

"So," I say, "tell me what it is I can do for you."

"I need a map. I would like to know about the next earthquake in California. The next big one."

"I'm following."

"I would like to know the exact time of the exact day and exact effected places. Just how accurate are you?"

I laugh and lean back in my chair. "Alan. There aren't many seers who can come close to what I can do. Earthquakes are tricky, though. You cannot read a fault line, but the lives can be read. I will have to follow lead upon lead and echo upon echo to get the kind of information you're talking about. I'll have to see people read news reports that will affect other people, over and over again to get accurate information."

"Can it be done?"

"Of course it can," I tell him. "But the price isn't going to be pretty."

"How much?"

"I couldn't tell you that right now, Alan. I couldn't begin to estimate."

This time, he laughs. "You're telling me that you can see an earthquake from the future by not a price tag?"

"I'm telling you that I am selective about what I tell my clients. Especially those who come unannounced. I will work on this and find out how much work it will be and that is how I will arrive at the figure which I can already see. But I insist on going about that by the natural means."

"When?"

I close my eyes. "Two months. Almost two months. Come back on the 10th of February." Things will be more settled by then, I think to myself. Though this isn't the high order that I've made it out to be, negotiating work with having a new girl in the house is going to take some getting used to.

Abigail Winters

November 16th, 2006

Derek has been distracted these last few nights. Or the last week or so. I'm not sure how far into being distracted he was when I started to notice. I only have one or two nights off from work a week, and I usually spend it with Derek at the Café Andante. We sit and drink coffee, forever talking circles around what it is that's on our minds when we're together. It doesn't matter what it is that we talk about, just so long as it's not his brother. I think we both feel better that way; it's healing to talk to each other.

It's silly, really. I doubt we'd have much in common with each other; if it weren't for his brother, we'd never be friends. But I find more and more that Derek is my one connection still remaining with Vic, and that alone makes him worth the time.

But these last two weeks, or a month, but probably closer to two weeks, it hasn't been his brother that's been distracting Derek. It's been images

50

of whatever pretty little girl it is that he has been visiting at the bookstore. He comes wondering over from the bookstore on Olive just a twittering with a lost look in his eyes. And he always comes over, huffs down into his chair, and says, "Sorry. I'd be here earlier, but I was over at the bookstore." His hands go up and rub his face like he is just so burdened with affection that he has to sort through.

The truth is, I know how he feels because he looks exactly like I used to. He looks burdened and stressed and distracted like I used to. And it's sad to watch someone like that and sadder that he won't just open up his mouth and start talking about the whole thing. Instead I watch him mull it all over and over in his head, wondering how he's going to come to terms with the whole thing. And he keeps up his side of the conversation with me pretty well, but all the while his eyes are lost in a pantheon of thought.

We don't talk about much. His school, my job. TV shows. Just a bunch of talk that doesn't get anywhere near the truth of anything. But the company is nice. And everything stays simple, never going in to what was before.

Now I see his shadow sprawled out in front of him, dragging him down the sidewalk towards the café. His hands are deep in the pockets of his coat, no doubt cold as anything. His head is down, watching his feet, probably making sure he doesn't step on any cracks, or counting the number of footsteps in each square of cement.

"Hey," he says sitting down.

"What's up?" I say. "Are you going to buy anything?" I motion to the inside of the café.

"I don't know. Do you want to move inside? It's pretty freaking cold out here."

"Nah."

"C'mon."

"It's not so bad under the heater. Go get a cup of coffee and you'll think it's summer."

He finally lumbers down into his seat. I pull a Cloves cigarette out of my pack and fish for the lighter in my purse.

"Oh. So this is why we're outside. So you can work on your new habit."

"It's not so new a habit. I've been doing it since I moved out of Dad and Terri's house."

"How is the new place, anyway?"

"Good. Too big. We talked about this two nights ago, Derek. Don't you remember? The one room is totally empty? I was thinking about getting a cat?"

Derek sinks down into his seat and sighs. "Sorry, Abbie."

"What's the big deal with her anyway?"

Shock registers on his face. "Who?"

"Don't give me that shit, Derek. It's been weeks. Or maybe even a month or so. The girl in the bookstore. Whoever the hell it is that you go visit before coming here every night."

"Well, I wouldn't say that I visit her."

"Jesus, Derek. You stalking her?"

"No. I like the bookstore anyway. I spend a lot of time there anyway."

"I'm just trying to figure this whole thing out," I say. "I keep wondering why you haven't brought her up to me. It is a *her*, right?"

He smirks at me, like I have no place suggesting such a thing. "I don't know," he makes one of those half-smiling frowny faces. It gives the impression of *I'm being serious but I'm going to go ahead and act like I'm half-kidding just for the hell of it to protect my ego.* "I mean, we've been hanging out a lot and, you know, I don't want to hurt—"

"Jesus Christ, Derek. You think you're going to hurt *my* feelings?"

His body takes the *awe, shucks* posture. "Well, I don't presume."

"Then don't, Derek."

"I mean, we've been hanging around a lot. We've

been spending a lot of time together. You never thought about it?"

"I don't know, Derek. You're so young. It never crossed my mind."

"Yeah, those two years are like two canyons between us."

"Shut up. You know what I mean." And I realize that he does, in fact, know what I mean. That I see him as the little brother. I walked right into it, violating our silent agreement not to bring *him* up. To not talk about *before*.

"It wouldn't be so stupid," Derek is looking down, like the ashtray on the table is fascinating or something, "for you to like me."

"No," I mirror his now quiet tone. "It wouldn't be stupid. After all, you're really helped me to put my life back together. I don't mean that you aren't great or anything, Derek. It's just not the circumstances that I look for in a relationship."

Derek shakes his head and looks up to meet my eyes. "No. Our lives aren't back together, Abbie. We're just going through the motions. So don't fool yourself."

"Derek, that's all there is. There are only motions to go through. We just didn't realize that before."

Before. Jesus. Before. Here we are talking about it.

"When my mom died, Derek, I was able to

convince myself that there was still a lot of meaning left in my life. I was able to go on because for God's sake, I was so young and, after all, we knew she was dying."

"Does that make it easier?"

"It let me insulate myself to some degree. And we got to talk about it together and she had such a positive view of the whole thing.

"But," I continue, noticing there are no tears on my face. "I also had your brother. You remember that I stayed in your house for a week while my dad dealt with everything?"

"Yeah."

"I never realized how much he meant. Only now do I see it. And thank God you came around here that night. Thank God you've helped me navigate through this whole thing with him not around to distract me. Thank God I can go through the motions again."

"Yeah," he says again. "You too. I mean, my school stuff has really suffered. It's not like my parents have been on my ass to finish my homework or anything like that. And I've just kind of become the quiet guy in class. The guy who everyone knows is carrying around this baggage."

We both sit quietly, going over the ramifications of talking about things so honestly and bluntly. We've strayed far from his stalking, and I don't know how to guide the conversation back in that direction. I'm glad to not know what he's thinking about right now, as he looks down lost in thought. How hard it must be for him, waking up every day to the absence in his house. I think about how that absence reflects itself in me. Vic gone. And shortly after that, how Erica moved away, leaving me alone with my dad and step-mom, both of whom I feel like couldn't wait for me to move out so they could recapture their puppy-love together."

And I think about how I lost my religion. How long it's been since I've felt connected to anything. And yet here is this boy looking for the same things I am. I've known him for so long and never really looked at him until his brother died. He's an echo from my past, all that feels left of who I was. And he doesn't seem real. Not even these last four or five months that we've been hanging out, coping with things through the minor distraction that we each provide the other. I want to reach over and hold the fingers poking through his jacket sleeve, but I just can't. I look at his face in the shadows, and find that I'm glad that we're being honest with each other. Maybe this is a new step. Maybe we can actually move ahead. Or move, at least.

"I want to show you something, Derek," I break

the silence. I stand up and move around the table to the chair directly next to him.

Derek Neely

November 16, 2006

She whispers: "I want to show you something, Derek."
Abbie pulls the chair next to me over so it's only inches
away from mine. She's facing me now, sitting down
and very close. Like in my personal space close.

"Hold on," she says, as if I'm getting impatient
with her sitting so closely. She looks down at her shirt
and her fingers find the buttons on her blouse, and I'm
a little shaken when they start fumbling the top few
buttons loose.

About a thousand thoughts are racing through my
head right now as she spreads open her shirt. I can't
think of what to say, and I start looking around to see if
anyone else out on the patio is staring at us. I feel a
hand on my face and it turns my head to look at Abbie
again.

"Here," she says quietly. "Look."

Her fingers trace scars that adorn her body from
her collarbone to above her bra. Each one is a

randomly placed rift about an inch and a half long, sprinkled like pepper over her pale skin.

"What the hell?" I finally squeeze out. "What happened?"

"These," she start, "Are from me." Her fingers linger on the marks as she starts to pull her shirt back together. "They are part of me, Derek. Part of my life for the past year or so."

I don't know what to say and my mind pulls me in several directions; to touch the scars myself; to button her up and hold her close; to rip the shirt off. The look on my face must convey my confusion.

"I'm a cutter," she says, as if answering a question that I didn't articulate. "Besides talking to you, this is the only way that I have to deal with everything. It moves the pain from inside to the outside."

She sits back in her chair, fully clothed now. She lights a long paper-bag colored cigarette.

"Why?"

She shrugs.

"Haven't you heard of crying? Isn't that what crying is supposed to be all about? Expressing sadness?"

"Shit, Derek. I've cried till I was numb. Don't let this make things weird."

"All about Vic?"

59

"Vic, my dad, Erica moving away, the loneliness I've felt since I stopped practicing my religion, oh, and let's not forget the whole Mom dying when I was 12 thing, Derek. My whole life is made up of things to cry about. I'd never be able to get out of bed it I cried about it all."

I can see the tears she's holding back now. She drags from the cigarette and closes her eyes. Her eyelids push a shallow moisture down her cheeks. She breathes out and sucks in her breath quickly, looking at me with wide, vulnerable eyes. Something about this scene makes me want to hold her face tightly in my neck.

I think I feel the second hand on my watch tick forward. Everything around us is filtered out and it's like I'm sitting on an empty patio with this sad girl, my dead brother's ex-girlfriend. Her smoke breezes past my face and it smells sweet and spicy, like a cabinet in my grandmother's house in New Mexico.

"When did this start?" I finally ask her.

She takes another deep breath. She sighs. "Oh, around the time Vic died. It pulls me up, though, Derek. It does. And who cares if—"

"I care. I care, Abbie, shit. I care."

"You care if my body is scratched up under my clothes?"

"I care if you're hurting yourself. Christ." I slump down in my chair. "Jesus."

"Sorry, Derek," she sounds less sad and more peeved. "I wouldn't have told you anything if I knew it was going to be such a burden for you."

"Have you talked about this with anyone? I mean, you probably should be seeing someone about all these issues, right? They have doctors for this, Abbie. It's a revolting thing to do to yourself."

Her eyes narrow and whatever vulnerability I thought I saw in them a few minutes ago is totally dead. Now her defenses are up and she's on the warpath.

"Fuck, Derek. Just fuck, you know? I wasn't looking for you to solve my issues here. I don't need you're fucking advice. I should see someone? Yeah, you think? Thanks, Frued. Thanks fucking Einstein, you're the goddamn best."

Her hand snaps her purse up as she straightens her legs to stand. She flicks her half a cigarette into the parking lot. She storms off.

For a minute I have this terrible selfish thought that now I'm free to go back to the bookstore. But before I can even think that thought through to its obviously hostile conclusion, I'm trying to catch up with Abbie. I start to call something out, like I'm sorry, but I know that's not what she's looking for. She's power walking down Olive with storefronts lighting the sidewalk in front of her when I finally decide what to say.

"I was going to kill myself," I blurt out.

She stops.

"Abbie, I was going to."

She looks at my eyes.

"It's been over a year. You realize that, don't you?"

Her voice is soft. "Of course I fucking realize that, Derek. Of course."

"I decided I'd give myself a year. One year. That if I couldn't deal with it by then, I'd go for it. I'd be dead."

She's close to me now. Back in the whole personal space thing. I feel her hand on mine.

"And I was pretty well resolved on that."

"What happened?"

"We started talking. And I realized that I didn't have to be able to deal with it. Things go and go and fucking go no matter if we deal with it or not."

Her face is soft curves in the streetlight. Her blonde hair looks almost orange under the lights. "Don't say 'fuck,' Derek. It's not you."

I smile. "So I understand, Abbie. I understand about the cutting."

"I never should have told you."

"No," I realize that we are squeezing each other's hand. "No, I'm glad you did. It's just, you know, I thought that maybe you were okay. Or that you were going to be okay. Or something."

"And I won't be."

"And you won't be."

We walking away form the Andante, towards the center of Mission Square.

"And now there's this girl," Abbie says. "And maybe that's something."

"I doubt it. I don't think she's so much as noticed me. You want to come? To the bookstore? You could see her? Give me your opinion?"

"No, no, Derek. It's won't look good, me walking in there with her."

"C'mon."

"I'll see her if she becomes significant, Derek. What's her name?"

"Damned if I know."

"Shit, Derek, really? You don't know the name of the girl you're stalking?"

"Just come."

"Actually," she stops walking. "I kind of have somewhere I have to be right now."

My face probably looks like a question mark.

"It's an appointment. It's no big thing."

"At 9:30?"

"Shit, is it 9:30 already?"

"Almost."

We hug. We hug pretty tight and pretty close. We hug often enough, but this is the first time that we hug and I feel like I'm pressed against a topography of scars hidden underneath four layers of clothes. We let go.

She crosses the street and I watch her. She yells out that she has another night off in a couple nights. She'll be at the Andante. I decide not to go to the bookstore, but to watch where she goes. I don't know why, but I do.

She walks into a building on the other corner of Mission Square, the place where she works, Stones. It's a bar and it's pretty busy, but I know she has the night off. I walk closer. I notice a shadow moving in the window upstairs above the bar, just behind the neon sign. It's a psychic shop above the bar, and the sign looks like a huge eye looking out over the square. Martin Delphi, it reads.

I just can't tell if it's her up there or not. None of my business.

chapter 3

Tydomin White

December 22, 1997

Last night was just like I thought it would be. The babysitter came and Mom and Dad kissed me goodbye. I hugged them. I felt Dad, how big his chest is, with my head pressed against him. I listened to his breath. I heard his heart.

I put my face deep into Mom's neck. I breathed with my nose so I could smell her skin. I wanted to breathe it in and not let it out; to keep her in my body.

I didn't cry. I never cry when something sad is about to happen. When I look back later, I can feel how sad it was. But I can't feel sad or happy about anything before it happens. It isn't fair. I know it, but I can't feel it.

I know that it upsets Mom and Dad when I tell them what will happen. They don't mind as much when I look back. Like when I told Mom about her horse show and how proud grandma was. She as surprised, maybe a little scared, and even though she was crying, I don't think she was sad. I was sorry I told her, all the same.

When I first saw this, the accident, I decided to keep it to myself. I look my picture of it and threw it in the fireplace when they weren't looking. I watched it burn and felt relieved when all of its smoke went up the chimney.

I let out my breath, my breath filled with Mom, when they walked out the door and Kelly locked it behind them. I turned it around and I was coloring when I heard the car start. I colored a picture of my rabbit that the Easter bunny gave to me when I was five. When I heard the car drive away, I wanted to move my legs as fast as they could go to the door and run out and stop them. But it was too late and I knew it was too late several days ago.

When Kelly put me to bed, she said, "You were quiet tonight, Ty."

"There's nothing to talk about yet."

"Well, there's no talking now. It's bedtime."

"We'll talk later, Kelly."

I sat awake in my bed, dreading all the talking I was going to have to do. I waited until the police lights lit up my room, then I grabbed my rabbit and walked in my PJs to the living room. I went over it so many times in my head that I only knew I was doing it for real when I felt butterflies in my stomach.

"Ty," Kelly said, squatting down to look in my eyes. "Something really bad has happened," she said.

I looked at the officer. He was sad. He held his squarish blue hat under his arm. I could feel that he was sad and I could feel what he had seen. I thought I would draw him later, making that face at the seven year-old orphan whose parents he had just tried to save.

I wanted to tell everyone that it was alright. I already knew, please don't be sad telling me. But all of a sudden, when the started to talk, I started to cry. The tears welled up and dripped down my face and I heard my own choking breath. So I sat down to hear what everyone wanted to tell me.

"Wait," I told the officer between sobs. "You need to call an ambulance. Kelly is going to pass out soon." And before the confused look on his face turned into surprise, Kelly fell over on the ground, white as a ghost. She couldn't watch, I suppose.

Now I'm in an office. CPS. There are phone calls being made. They know my parents had no will. My parents' friends hardly know me; I was kind of a secret because of the things I might say, always kept out of sight. I tell them I have an uncle named Red who lives in the mountains. I haven't seen him for a while and I don't know his number but will they please find it. He will take care of me, I tell them, if they can just give him a call.

The lady helping me is named Samantha. I look back at her life to distract myself from what's going on in my life. She had her heart broken years ago and she lives alone. Her care isn't fake, like Dr. Torrance's was. She has seen lots of kids like me, kids who find themselves alone, and she always feels bad for them. She always wants them home.

On her desk is a picture of kids. They're in Mexico, poor kids who have nothing. Every year for the last four, she has gone to help these kids. I feel bad for her. How she always needs to help kids. How she will never have any. I don't tell her these things, about how she will never have kids, because I don't know if she knows this yet. I realize that there is tragedy everywhere when a life is looked at from all these sides; frontward backwards, past and future. Sad.

My bunny is making me sad. I didn't think it would, but it is. I would have left it at home if I thought it would make me cry. I remember all the times Dad put it in my bed at night. I see the way Mom set it up at the table for breakfast. And it's all sad.

I started home schooling when I got bunny. School

wasn't a right fit for me. The teacher said that I was precocious and that I had no sense of urgency. She said that I had no drive, I was very distracting and disruptive with my pictures and the things I would say. So bunny was my classmate at home. And that makes me sad.

No matter how many poor kids get houses because of Samantha, her job makes her sad. She will be sad when she has no kids of her own.

"We've spoken to your uncle," Samantha tells me a couple hours later, waking me up from the couch. "He's getting everything together and he'll be here tomorrow morning." She doesn't smile, but her face is bright.

"You're doing a good job, Samantha."

"Oh, you are, honey. You're doing a great job with all of this stuff." She explains to me that she is a professional councilor that she is there for me to talk to. That if I want, she will call Dr. Torrance and he can come talk to me, too.

"No thank you," I say. "I would rater not talk to Dr. Torrance ever again."

"Would you like to talk to me?"

I think about this for a second. Yes, I would like to talk to her, but I can see that I won't. I don't want to alarm her about how different I am. I don't want her to

study me the way that Dr. Torrance did. Our two
meetings every week, looking back them and feeling
them, I can see they were really for him; for him to
study me.

I would like to tell Samantha about how I feel,
being alone, being an orphan, having a stranger who I
already know coming to take care of me. But I cannot
take out the complexities of what I am, of how I see
and know things. I don't want to scare her. I don't
want to be looked at that way. And I can't answer the
question of how a normal girl would see this. So I don't
try.

"No, thank you, Samantha," I say. "I don't think
that I am ready."

There's a sad look in her face when she pats my
leg. The way she looks at Bunny makes me thing for a
minute that she can feel things about people's past,
too. Then I realize it's probably just a detail that makes
me more real to her.

There was a boy who she helped a few years
ago that really changed her. His dad beat him. He was
wearing a Batman shirt. And I can feel through
Samantha that when she looked at the boy in the
Batman shirt, that little detail ended up hurting her.
Her emotions dwelled on it for a long time—that in this
boy's troubled life, with his dad beating him and his

mother dead from an overdose, him locked in the bathroom for a week—he had time to like Batman. She was overwhelmed. It was the one little thing that made him like the other boys his age, the one thing that made him seem human. And how could a human go through all he's gone through?

Samantha is interesting. She takes care of kids and carries parts of them away with her. She doesn't mean to. If I could tell her about my ability to see someone's past, she'd be glad she didn't have it. It would tear her apart. She is typing something up, so I am not asked any question for a while. I look back at her life to try and understand her better. Anything to keep me from looking at last night.

Suddenly, I have a very strange sort of *déjà vu*. She helped a boy at some kind of hospital. An older boy, just a few days ago. He was blind and, she thought, crazy. She wanted to teach him to read Braille. He laughed at this and his laugh scared her. He said that he knew what she was thinking; the idea of helping him was beyond God, so who did she think she was?

The *déjà vu* part was that I can see this boy in the future. I'm going to meet him. I'm pretty sure it's the same boy, just grown up a little. And he laughs at the saddest things. He's far off in the future, in the part that is really cloudy for me. I wouldn't have seen him at all, I think, except that her memories jogged my mind.

What are those? Reverse memories?

I think about telling Samantha about it. But I can see that I don't. Sometimes I have to remember just to take my time. Everything will be here without me pushing it. So I try to bury it down without thinking too much about last night.

Martin Oaks

October 11, 2006

You might not believe this, but I still go to Mass every Sunday. Like anything else in my world, it sickens me a great deal. Most those surrounding me in the service have minds that wander to laundry piles gathering dust at home to sports stadiums in far-off cities. Like so many channels paging through the catalogue of vile lugubrious drivel, looking for something to sedate the worldly mind, these churchgoers wonder around in thoughts to pass the time and tedium of yet another service. And, so my mind wanders, looking for one single pious soul.

Why do these people come? I always wonder. To be seen. To feel forgiven. To appease someone else. I cannot understand these motivations. My stomach turns at the thought.

I search the crowd for someone humble who begs their Lord for forgiveness and mercy. I flip through the pages until I find a mind who looks up at their God and feels the pain and intolerance of their own unworthiness. Once I find this vessel of the Lord, I indulge in their thoughts, having found my own sedative.

Nothing calms my mind and stops the infinite search for a tangible identity like the petitions of a pious mourner of the human condition. The Spirit breathes the thick smoke into my head and I scrape the insides of their mind for thoughts of penance and self-loathing. I adopt these pities. Their cries for peace and security I enjoin. Their solemn vows to live life with integrity and dedication to The Almighty sooth whatever it is I have in place of a soul.

When I was young, my mom threw me in an institution in Merced. She wanted to be rid of me and she told me that they would help me there. It was in this institution that I learned to love the pain and suffering going on in the minds of people. There was one man in particular. He was an older man who would play the piano every evening. He never spoke, not even once. The nurses and doctors thought his mind was far off, never going to come back to him. But I found solace in that mind.

He played the piano and thought of his son. His son was something like me, someone he couldn't understand. Just like how my mom treated me, this man got rid of his son. He put him in an orphanage when he was 10, gave him up. He couldn't cope with the burden of this child. He taught his son piano, and only in playing piano could he ever communicate with his son. He had heard different things; his son was autistic, he was schizophrenic, he was psychic. He just couldn't deal with it any more.

And now, years and years later, he couldn't deal with what he had done. He all but lost his mind in lamenting his past actions. It was sweet, sweet paradise to hear this man beg forgiveness with ever press of the piano keys. It was so wonderful to see someone feeling so horrible about something they never should have done. He deserved this pain, and he never realized that this pain was the tool of forgiveness.

Few churchgoers ever find peace and happiness or atonement with the Lord. Yet I find the at-one-ness I seek in the tormented yearning of a corporeal soul in pain. For the brief flicker of a moment, I become real to myself, I feel what they feel and it is a strong and true likeness of what I should feel like living the life that I do. I have a conscience. I have an identity. I have self, real and acute.

I walk out of the hallowed doorway and down the steps to Mission Square a saved man.

Promptly, that forgiveness is lost. Again I join the myriad of other people in Ashlan whom hope to quell their hearts' wandering with other vices. I have no choice but to encompass these petty feelings.

That is, at least, my usual Sunday. That is the day that I look forward to most, knowing that whatever else I go through that week, whatever else I see, no matter who enters my shop and no matter what it is that I tell them in order to rob them blind, there is a light ahead. There is a moment of pain and forgiveness. With that knowledge, that confidence that I will wash myself in atonement, I can rest comfortably in the moral ambiguity of my survival.

But this happy trend has come to a sad ending. The comfort I have taken for so long in the assurance of a peaceful mind has been shattered. These brief shinning moments in the infinity of other have been robbed by the abomination that calls himself a priest.

He's been here for a few months, the false father. It took weeks for me to wander into his mind. And it wasn't the first time that I filled my head with his smoke that I noticed the ways that he lead us all astray. But once I was there at the proper time, I have forever had my peace and complacence sullied.

I was having a particularly hard time finding the proper vehicle of forgiveness within the large congregation. This is almost never the case, since the chapel is so large and, being a historic mission, pious souls come from all over to experience the word of their Lord in our hall. But on this particular day, no one mind was in the proper state of prostration. None of the general congregation nor of the visitors to our hall were in the proper state for prayer. Never had I seen such a high level of distraction exhibited by so many.

There must be an underlying cause, I reasoned. I searched and searched and found no commonalities between the clouds of distraction. I surmised that the vantage of the priest might give me further insight.

I moved my mind to join his, a ghost slinking between the souls in the pews. The Spirit breathed the smoke of the priest's mind until it clouded my head.

I looked out along with the priest at the sizable congregation gathered in the fold. The faces stared diligently at the priest, as if they were trying their hardest to take part in the conversation with God going on. I could see nothing that gave the slightest clue of distraction or discontent. But the priest's gaze kept on drifting. The eyes of our Shepard kept fluttering upon one object in the large room.

And what was it that this abomination of the Lord kept staring at? What was so valuable to his eyes and his conscience that he would take himself away from this holy hour to indulge in? It was the barely visible pair of panties being worn by a 12 year-old girl.

There are few people who would be able to imagine the level at which my blood began to boil. This is why the congregation is still lost in the wandering thoughts of the mundane world. You have to understand. This is not a man up on a stage reciting the words of poetry or literature, throwing out images and rhymes for the congregation to ponder intellectually. This is the vessel of God to these poor people.

As Jesus laid his hands upon Paul, so Paul laid his hands upon his disciples. So the Pope has laid his sanctity on this priest. As so are we *all* touched by God through this messenger. However distant that may seem, this is a direct flow of energy from The Almighty to the souls of those present.

And this man creates a broken circuit.

There is no other way to see this. This priest is betraying these people and their God by preventing their connection with the perverse. I stayed in his mind as he flippantly stared at this girl's white underwear with pink dots. I felt his mouth water as he took longer and longer glances. Even as he spoke—merely mouthing—the words of his cuckold God, his erection pressed against his pants.

I closed my eyes, blocking access to the priest's vision and opening the doors to his mind. The smoke changed to the images and sounds of his min. He was thinking, in great detail, of pulling the girl's skirt off, slipping off her panties and burying his face between her legs.

I was shocked. I could feel the blood and color flush from my face. Were these memories or only a fantasy? The difference between the two possibilities is ethereal for this deluded audience, but of the utmost concern for the life of this young girl.

I opened my eyes. I saw that still he gazed at this girl and I could not tell what regard she looked at him. I shifted my gaze. I moved it gently the 20 or so feet to the mind of the girl's. The Spirit moved the smoke to take the shape of her mind. I could tell that she was unaware of her panties. She was not even looking at the priest, but over his head to the stained glass portrait of the virgin. I closed my eyes and saw that she was thinking of school, home, and some TV show which had nothing to do with church. As hard as I tried, I could not locate any living memories she might well have of this priest in such a private setting.

There was not much room for relief. Though I was happy to see that he didn't harm the child, he was still breaking the bond between these people and their

God for the simple perversion and gratification of the senses. I did not know what to do about it. I canceled all my appointments for the next two days to contemplate how I was going to rid our church of this evil man.

And today I woke up and had three cups of coffee before leaving my apartment. I walk up the steps to the church with a lump in my throat for what I am about to do. I know the schedules of the priests at the church like the touch of my hands. There are not many people in or around the church at this time, so I am very nervous about being able to borrow the right perceptions to successfully navigate my way through the church with little assistance from the sight of others and into the confessional booth.

The door opens quietly and I feel my way to the padded kneeler and listen to the wooden sliding door open and suddenly I see myself out of the corner of the priest's eyes filtered through wooden slats. I bow my head low, wanting to hide my face at least to some degree.

The priest's voice breaks the silence, "Yes?"

"I am here for the sacrament of Penance. O God, I am heartily sorry for the sins I have committed."

"Continue."

"I have raped a child of 12," I say quietly.

82

"I see."

I pause for some moments, begin to speak, then stop, as if searching for words. I wring my hands, gulp dryly and enjoy these moments of his attention. I want him to feel the tension within himself through me, his vessel. "And in doing so, I have betrayed not only her, but my God. And more, I have betrayed hundreds of humble worshipers."

A sort of a *humm* sounds in his throat.

There is quiet between us again. I search his mind, paging through his wandering thoughts, hoping to find a well of guilt. He was hiding it from himself, convinced that he was no offender himself. I had to probe him further.

"Her name is Mary Alger. She is the daughter of Tom and Alice who have been attending service since I've come to this church. Some Sundays, she wears a skirt so short, I can look up her legs and straight into heaven." Now I let my voice climb out of the soft tone of one seeking forgiveness and I let lechery come through. I search his mind as it races to understand my thoughts and I see many more girls from the service that he has violated with his mind.

For a moment, I am shocked. I see in his mind a girl over whom he has lusted not in the church, but in some kind of a store. She is standing behind the counter punching buttons into a register. The priest's gaze lingers on the girl's breasts. And though she is a couple years older than I remember her—and older than most of the girls in his mind—I know exactly who she is.

"Tydomin," I whisper to myself. I can see through his eyes that he has turned to look at me, wondering what I had said. "And she is not the only one," I continue loudly. "I have made a practice of looking over the congregation and finding the girls who are just beginning to sprout. Girls whose bodies are new to them, strange, exciting. Do you know what I'm talking about?"

His voice is shaken, "I believe so." He's coming around now, starting to open up to his guilt.

"My hands grace their bodies, their young and blossoming bodies. I run my fingers over their skin and slip them under their clothes. Oh God, how they moan for my touch. How my mouth waters at the thought."

He says nothing, but begins to damn himself inwardly. He *knows* this is what he's wanted. He's been thinking about it for so long, it's been like background music in his mind for the last several years, everywhere he goes. And now that barrier in his mind—the one that so many have that divides a person's mind, keeping who they are separate from

84

who they *think* they are—is close to coming down

"Don't you see, Father? Don't you see that I am a demon soul, misleading the entire church and god for my own gratification with these who are God's innocents? But there are none truly innocent, are there Father? Secretly, in their hearts, then have yearning that they cannot contain. They lust for me and I know it."

"They do not." He sounds near tears. Then, "Who are you?"

"I am a priest, Father, that is all you need to know. I used to be like you. I used to merely look out on the congregation and think these thoughts. It was a betrayal of my God and a misleading of my people. So there is nothing more wrong with what I do now. How I lure them away from their families, get them alone, bless them with my touch and with guilt."

"Stop! Stop, Demon!"

"You have the gall to call *me* a demon? We are guilty of the same sins, are we not?"

"We are not!"

"You say that with the same tongue you thrust up the skirts of children? You think this is somehow *normal*? Like this is something that the Lord will ever forgive of you?" Now I see images in his mind that I cannot tell if they are fantasy or memory. Have there

been other girls who he has slept with? I cannot know.
It doesn't matter.

"He will. He does."

"He does nothing of the sort. You have taken
creations of his and spent their innocence in your
mind. You have made their salvation impossible these
past many weeks, thanks to the profound weakness in
your heart. You have tormented their sleep, given
them to Satan without so much as a choice." My voice
rises. "Your demon spirit sleeps in their beds and
dirties their sheets and you think that you can tell me
who is forgiven? You are the messenger of Evil. You
haven't even confessed these sins yourself and you sit
here and listen to *me* do it."

"It cannot be," he whispers, "I am so sorry."

"You will never preach here again."

"Never. Never, I swear."

"I don't care where you go, what you do. There is
no salvation for you; you cannot be reformed. You
cannot be saved."

"Never. I know this."

"But if you leave this mission, I will never tell a
soul what I know."

"Thank you. Oh Lord, thank you." He falls into
tears.

"God the Father of mercies, through the death and

resurrection of His Son, has reconciled the world to himself and sent the Holy Spirit among us for the forgiveness of sins; through the ministry of the Church may God give you pardon and peace, and yet," I pause. "I cannot absolve you from your sins. In the name of the Father, and of the Son, and of the Holy Spirit, I damn you to hell eternal."

Quickly I stand up and leave the confessional. There are not enough eyes around for too safe a passage out of the church, but I rush as fast as I can, navigating by memory. Just as I step out of the door, the priest catches a glimpse of my back. I step into the outside and take a deep breath. I cannot tell if I am more revolted or excited. Adrenaline rushes through my blood.

I don't think he'll ruin another Sunday for me.

But Tydomin. I had I assumed she died in the fire. What the priest saw of her must have been after the fire, she was older and the priest hasn't lived in Ashlan long enough. I wonder if she managed to keep her Daddy's secrets.

Red Scabergrade

December 23, 1997

My hand is cramped from all the papers I have to sign. The room is shallow and Christmas music plays on computer speakers on a far off desk. There've been so many sympathetic nods and half-smiles that I have to hold back from rolling my eyes when it happens again. The office is used to dealing with orphans, but it is rare for a child to lose both parents in this small town. They are thorough and it is tedious. Seven years of planning and these past few hours seem t have taken so much longer.

The last of the paperwork that I signed was as Tydomin's guardian. I authorized her family's possessions to be liquidated, their accounts emptied, and for it to be put into a trust fund for the girl.

At last they lead the girl out from the back. She is carrying a suitcase, a backpack, and a ratty stuffed rabbit. "Hi Red," she says, not quite looking up at me. Exhausted, the poor thing.

"Hi Tydomin," I say. "I'm very sorry about your parents."

She nods. She's tired of being around all these people. In a few months' time, she will come to tell me how rarely she was around strangers growing up. How her confused abilities made for awkward experiences for her parents. How these last two days have been baffling, surrounded by sympathetic people she has never met. She doesn't seem to be relieved to see me except that I'm taking her away from here.

As for now, I can only wonder if she is able to make any sense of any of this at all. I take her bags and lead her to the truck.

Abigail Winters

November 18, 2006

The stairs up to this guy's place are narrow, like against building code narrow. I don't know how these places get away with it. The lighting is so bad that it just compounds the whole narrow step problem and you have to hold on to the handrail for dear life. Every time I go up these stairs, I wonder who else has gone up them and what they had smeared all over their hands and how many times I'll have to wash mine before I can trust them with something like food again.

The hallway is dark leading up to his door; one little low-wattage bulb sticks out of the wall, void of any kind of shade. The door is narrow, too. If you saw me coming here in a movie, you'd be shouting at me to not be stupid, to turn around. There is a sign on the door, just like the neon one outside: an eyeball with the words "Martin Delphi" scripted around it. It's cheesy and all, but man is this guy ever good.

I knock. The door opens.

"Abigail. Good to see you again." Martin is a few years older than me, I think. I can't really tell. I've probably never seen a more nondescript guy in my whole life. If he snatched your purse in the middle of the mall, you wouldn't know what to tell the cops. He's regular looking. Normal looking, like Adam must have been. His skin is somewhere in between Norway and India, his hair light brown cut like a 10 year-olds, and always this dumb blue T-shirt and jeans. Always.

"Hi, Martin," I say. "I did what you said."

"Good, good. Come on in and let's talk."

Martin's shop is about what you'd expect a psychic shop to look like. It's dark, the lights trying hard to resemble candle flames, with lost of softness all around you. There are pillows to sit on around a low table in the middle of the room. There are fabrics hanging from the walls. And behind the bead curtains covering the windows is the ever-present glow from the neon sign. And it smells like patchouli. One wall has a selection of herbs and salts that belongs in a magick shop, but he has told me repeatedly not to buy any of it. He's perceptive to the fact that I used to be Wiccan and that I know the difference between real and fake materials of that sort.

"Sit," he motions to a cushion, which I then sit on. "How did it go?" He takes the cushion across the low dark wood table.

"Well," I say. "It went very well."

"Expand."

"He's nice. I couldn't exactly tell if he was really my type or not, but he's nice."

"He was there, then?"

"Oh, yes, he was just where you said he would be. Same table, ordered the same drink. Everything. You're really amazing." Martin was a customer of mine downstairs at Stone's. He always had coffee and would just sit and do what I would call "people watching." But I'd been coming here to his shop for a few weeks or so. Though his prices are high, he's worth every penny. Two nights ago, in talking about issues over work and school possibilities and those types of things, he told me he saw a man in my life.

"He's perfect for you. Brian Cadwell. You'll wait on his table tomorrow night. Strike up a conversation and he'll stick around for you to get off work," he had said. And, of course, he was right.

Initially, I was a little suspicious. I had never talked to Delphi about any love interests or anything like that. And even though I asked him a lot of questions about pursuing college out of state and looking at work in different cities, he never once mentioned the idea that I might want to stick around because of a boy. And yet here he was saying that starting a relationship with this guy was what I should do.

It just came up, he told me, an opportunity. Time changes, he said, and I should adapt to it.

"Tell me more," he says.

"Well, there he was in the corner booth all by himself, reading *A Tale of Two Cities,* just like you said," I tell him. "And yeah, talk about good looking."

"I told you," Delphi says. "I'm glad that things are working out. This is going to be a big key for you."

"Well," I say hesitantly, "I just don't know. I mean, we seem to have a lot in common. And he seems great. It's just, I don't know Delphi, I've been thinking more and more about moving up to East Bay and really trying things out on my own."

"You shouldn't doubt this, Abigail. I know it sounds strange coming from our background and everything that I've advised you on, but the timing could be better."

As he says this, I try and imagine Brian moving to Berkley with me.

"He's just out of high school. He's not going to college. He'd follow you to the ends of the Earth, so I doubt that Berkley will be any big problem for him.

"But," I say, "Do I end up *marrying* the guy?" I can't imagine wasting my time in a relationship right now unless it was something that was very serious.

"You won't be wasting your time, if that's what you're worried about," Delphi says. "Seeing the future is a complicated matter, but this is crystal clear, Abigail. Like so much else in life, this is really an issue of faith; sometimes it takes a while before you fully understand why something is meant to be."

"Well, I trust you, Martin. I've never really been big on psychics before. The only person I've ever known who was a psychic—"

"Tydomin?" Martin is suddenly sitting erect and I have his full attention. "You know Tydomin?"

"Yes," I say. "How did you know?"

"You were with her *tonight*?"

"Yes."

"Fascinating," he says almost to himself. "How didn't I see this before? Where has that girl been hiding?"

I look at him as he seems lost in thought. "How do you know Tydomin?"

"Well," he says. "I don't know her that well. I saw her once in a while when she was growing up. I worked now and then with her father. Though, I guess it wasn't really her father." Now he doesn't look concerned or thinking all of a sudden, but has a bright and cheery smile. "None of this would interest you, I'm sure. Just an old friend."

"Well, she's a strange girl."

"You could say that."

We continue talking. Martin has been coaching me on how I can break into a job at a magazine that I love that's published in Berkley and how I can move up there without spending every single cent to my name. He's helped me see how I can leave a lot of my life here in Ashlan behind me. And now he's guiding me towards this relationship that he says is soon going to mean much more to me than I ever thought.

It feels like we are wrapping things up when he suddenly brings her up again. "How do *you* know Tydomin?"

"Well, she was my best friend's roommate."

"Erica?"

"Yes." I had forgotten that I had spoken about Erica quite a bit with Martin, especially at the beginning of our meetings. "She's young, still in high school. But she's emancipated or something and gets to live like a grown-up.

"A friend of mine and I meet at the Andante every night I have off. I was sitting there waiting for Derek tonight and she just showed up out of the blue. I hadn't talked to her since Erica moved away. She acted like it was no big thing and parked it with a cup of coffee. Then, of course, once Derek showed up, all hems and haws, I was more or less left out of the conversation. So maybe this whole thing with Brian does have some fortunate timing, you know?"

"You mentioned that she's a psychic as well?" Delphi said.

I think about this. "No, I don't think that I did mention that."

"But she is."

"That's what Erica told me. We've never talked about it."

"So she doesn't talk about it."

"Why are you so interested? You want me to tell her to come up and visit you?"

"No," he says. "As a matter of fact, do me a favor, Abbie. Don't tell her that I asked about her. I'd like to surprise her."

I nod. Our time is up so I stand to leave. I reach into my purse for the fifty dollars that I owe him.

"Don't worry about it tonight, Abbie," he says. "We don't usually meet twice a week. I just wanted to know how things went last night, really. And you've told me." He flashes that engaging smile again. When Martin smiles, you feel some kind of approval, like you're happy that you were able to make him happy. I feel somehow more satisfied that I've pleased him by meeting this Brian than I am happy to have met him for myself. The smile also makes me feel thanked for not being paid.

Derek Neely

November 18, 2006

I shuffle my feet against the sidewalk wrapped up tightly against the cold. All the storefronts along Olive are decorated for Christmas, and most of the lighting that leads me down the street is coming from the lights strung from the shops to the light poles. They have halos of light around each one shining through the fog. Right now I can see about a block in either direction; the fog has been a lot like this every night this week. I'm still skittish in the fog and rarely drive in it.

I'm disappointed because the girl wasn't working in the bookstore tonight. But then again, it might be a good idea for me not hang around and chicken out anyway. Abbie has the night off, so I'm headed to the Andante to sit and waste the time the best way we know how.

A block away, the Andante comes into view from

the fog. There are ten or twelve tables lining the sidewalk out in front of the café, most of them look taken. I scan the tables to see if Abbie got a hold of one for us. As I get closer, I can pick her out, Clove cigarette in hand, sitting at the table on the edge. But there's someone with her.

Abbie waves me over, and as I get closer, I see that she is sitting with the girl from the bookstore. And man, does that make me nervous as hell. My stomach turns over, filled with rocks.

"Derek," Abbie calls out, "I'd like you to meet Tydomin. Tydomin, this is Derek, your stalker." She beams a bright smile through the fog.

"Thank you for that exciting introduction, Abbie. I'm going to go kill myself now."

"It's okay," Tydomin says sticking her hand out. "I've seen you in the store a couple times. I thought I'd come buy you a cup of coffee."   The third seat at their table is already adorned with a cup of coffee, presumable for me.

I sit down and feel the mug, still hot. "Thanks," I say. I look over at Abbie and she rolls her eyes and shrugs. "So," I start awkwardly, "How are you ladies?" I can tell it was a stupid thing to say. "How do you know each other?"

"You remember Erica?" Abbie says.

"Of course. Well, I only met her a handful of times."

"Tydomin was her roommate."

I looked quickly at the girl. "How old are you?"

"I'm 16."

"Where do you go to school?"

"I don't, really. I mean, I'm home schooled. As an emancipated minor whose parents chose to home school, I have the option of continuing in a program through a high school. So I check in every month with Ruther High and pick up another packet of work."

"Jesus," I say. "I want to take part in that."

"It's a mountain of paper work. I wouldn't covet it." The girl is smiling brightly and seems almost giddy. It's some kind of disturbingly enthralling alternate universe where this girl I have a crush on likes me. Or else Abbie has put her up to this.

I take a sip of my coffee. "I'm going to get some cream," I say. "Abbie, would you like to also get cream?"

"Yeah, what the hell. I'm going to get cream, too." But Abbie didn't even bother to pick up her coffee mug to act like she was doing anything other than walking into the café with me to talk.

"What the hell?" I say once inside the doors.

"She's your girl, right?"

100

"Yeah, but what the hell?"

"She walked up, plopped down, said hi, and that she was waiting for you."

"Okay," I say, "but what the hell?"

"She's a strange girl, Derek. Very precocious. Kind of, I don't know, naïve about dealing with people. Erica talked about her like she was some kind of sheltered kid, never really been around people much. Good luck with her." Despite her cynicism, Abbie is beaming with giddiness about watching this whole thing. "But I'm kind of a third wheel. Or fifth wheel, whatever the term is. I'll get going."

"You can't just leave."

"I sure as hell can. I'm not going to stick around watching love blossom and shit," she can't hide her smile.

"I'm way too nervous. I can't possibly go out there and sit with her myself."

"Grow a pair, Derek. Jesus."

We leave the café without procuring the cream. When we walk back outside, Tydomin is still there, still smiling. I just can't help but feel like this is a lot of pressure that I'm not ready for. Whatever reason she's smiling for, I cannot imagine wiping it off her face with pure ineptitude.

"Hey," I say smoothly while we sit back down.

"Sorry about that, Tydomin," Abbie says. "We were just talking about the date that I had last night. We weren't talking about you at all."

"How did it go? The date?" Tydomin asks.

"Very well, thank you. We're going out again this weekend."

"What's his name again?" I ask.

"Brian. He works here, actually."

I know, know know know, she doesn't mean Brian Cadwell. Probably, I figure, she's just making something up to cover our awkward regrouping.

"But, speaking of doing totally different things than hanging out with the two of you, I'm going to go and do something totally different than hang out with the two of you. Have a nice night."

"Yeah," I say. "I might need to get going soon, too."

"Shut the hell up and sit down, Derek. He's fine, Ty. Just hit him over the head every time he starts being a chicken-shit." She winks at the girl and walks off.

"Hey," I call after her. "I want you to call me later. I want to hear more about this date of yours."

"Yeah, I'll call tonight," Abbie says. "I'll tell you about mine and you tell me about yours." Abigail disappears into the fog.

"So," I say to Tydomin. "What brings you here?"

"I'm going to be honest with you, Derek. I knew you wouldn't have to guts to talk to me in the store. And, honestly, it's kind of trashy picking up on the sales clerk who you're too scared to look in the face every time you buy a book. But I wanted to meet you."

"How did you know I'd be here with Abbie?"

Tydomin takes a drink from her own mug, which doesn't have coffee in it but something frothy. "Again, Derek, I'll be as honest as I can. I know who you are. I've known Abbie for a year or so, and I even met your brother a handful of times."

"Really?"

"Yes. And I'm sure you're sick to death of hearing this, but he was an enchanting person and I'm so, so sorry that he's gone."

I nod. Whenever someone young dies in this town, everyone knows about it. Everyone tries to take the tragedy as their own. So, yes, she's right. I'm sick to death of hearing it. It's either because she's so damn pretty or because she was actually sincere in saying it, but it didn't bother me so much. "Thanks," I say. "And since we are running with the whole honesty thing, I want to tell you that I was too scared to talk to you."

She smiles. She's a pretty girl with long brown hair pulled back into some kind of ponytail thing. Her eyes

are dark but seem to shine every time I see her.
Whenever I see her working, she wears these long
flowing skirts and a blouse that matches. She's angular
and her movements are smooth, like she's constantly
directing a choir. Sitting here in the foggy Christmas
lighting, she's even more beautiful.

I check my watch. I don't have to be home for a
few more hours. But I realize now that I have
absolutely nothing else to say to fill that time. I reach
for my coffee.

"Don't be nervous," she says. "Would you like to
go for a walk?"

"A walk? In the fog? Yes."

chapter 5

sol smith

Tydomin White

December 23, 1997

I walk past the big familiar stranger and get to the passenger side of the truck before he does. I'm not sure exactly what the impulse is, but I want to beat him there. He throws my suitcase in the back of the truck and we hop in.

I'm quiet in the truck, looking out the window. Its' a long ride, I know, so I don't see why I should rush the conversation. I will know Red for a long time, and though this is my first chance to feel his history, I don't. I feel funny about reading him. We'll be together for a long time and I feel icky about it, like I should let him tell me first. I don't know if I've ever had that notion before. Perhaps it's because he knows about my feeling abilities and the awareness of it makes it an invasion of privacy.

I watch as the buildings pass by. A mall. Shopping centers. A movie theater. Car lots. These businesses thin into apartments and those thin into suburbs. The homes give way to orchards. Oranges, almonds, then miles and miles of grapes. The rows of vines flicker across the window like an old movie. I press my fingers against the window, then drag them down to the door. This leaves four streaks on the glass slowly fade away. I let my eyes focus on the streaks, then, as the disappear, I see the flickering rows of grape vines again.

Finally the grapes fade away, leaving brown grass populated with sparse groves of trees covered in mistletoe. The grass as far as the eye can see is dead and brown. Golden, my mom would call it. She thought that California was a beautiful place, no matter where you lived in it and which season it was and how ugly the characteristics were. The Golden State.

The grade sharpens. The trees get taller, greener, and immense in population. Only now does Red talk to me.

"You're a very special girl, Tydomin." His voice is quiet and not focused on me, like he was almost talking to himself.

"Yes," I say. "And precocious."

He laughs a little. "Why is that?"

I look at him. "I'm intrinsically entangled with my future-self. Even times in the life that I cannot yet see,

I have stolen the vocabulary and much of the basic functional knowledge."

"I see," Red says without a hint of disbelief. "You know this because?"

"Because I will know it some day. And that is one of the pieces of knowledge that has flowed up river to me."

"Interesting," Red says. "You're very right, Tydomin. You know a lot about this already." I feel myself being proud. Like for some reason Red's approval feels good to me, even though I don't know him. "Seeing is an art that can be honed and perfected, Tydomin."

"And you can help me."

"And I can help you. How long did you know I was coming?"

"Do you know my answer?"

Red looks away from the road to give me a puzzled look. "What do you mean?"

"I mean, don't you know what I'm going to say? Why would you ask me a question if you already know what I'm going to answer?"

"Because, Tydomin," he says. "The only way that I can know your answer is if you give life to it. If you never answer, I will never know what it is you were going to say. Do you understand?"

"Hmm," I say. "I wondered how it would work. Both of us having the vision."

"I've known others. And I've learned that our conversations must be more or less normal, despite the content we may cover. I cannot finish your sentences unless I let you say them—or I would not know what you had to say."

"How frustrating. Try. Try and tell me the answer to your question. Tell me how long I've known about you coming."

Red looks at me out of the corner of his eye. "This is pointless, Tydomin. Can't you see that I would tell you that? Do you not see that this conversation ends with you telling me?"

I'll get a headache if I think about this for too long. I had never considered the circular traps that having two of us together would create. There's nothing normal or logical about how this works. I decide to give in.

"I've known you were coming for about two weeks," I say at last. "But I've known of you for years. Shadows of you, glimpses. I just didn't know how you would fit in."

"Very observant," he says. "Personalities come through before events if they interact with many events. But seeing the future isn't the only that sets you apart, is it Tydomin?"

"No," I say.

"You are a seer, like I am. But you are more than that."

"I don't know what to call my other ability."

"You are a feeler, Tydomin."

"A *feeler*," I say to hear myself say it, to make the word in my mouth.

"You feel the pasts of people. You feel the emotions they have about the events in their past, correct?"

"Yes," I say. "Have you met other feelers?"

"I have."

"What are they like?"

Red sighs. His eyes narrow. He looks like he's concentrating on the road, but he's really concentrating on the right answer. "The two sides of you should make for a very interesting dichotomy."

"Why?"

"I've never met or even heard of someone who is both a seer and a feeler. But I have known many from each group.

"Seers tend to be distant and serious people. Aloof. If they've tapped into their abilities at a young age, they are almost certainly precocious." He nods his head at me. "If they haven't had the proper upbringing or training, they often pay very little attention to the world around them. They live in the future and don't quite respect the present that is so transitory. They can be withdrawn. They are almost always emotionally ambivalent towards what it is that they see."

He gives me a glance as some kind of inquiry. He wonders with this glance how much of this description resonates with me. I nod and smile my response as much of it sounds familiar, like a horoscope reading of your sign. "And feelers?" I ask.

"Feelers are often the opposite, as you can imagine. They find emotional significance in the people around them. Motivation of character is obvious to them and they understand interpersonal relationships on many levels. They don't hold grudges, but they can hardly look back at the past without a hint of regret. They feel sorrow for the passage of events. They know that time ripens a moment until it is spoiled, merely by the distance of the event or the person that they are looking back at. They are empathic to almost everyone, no matter who they are.

"This presents a fault, very often. They have empathy for those who are 'bad' for them. They think that someone's direction in life can be changed through the understanding of why it is so. They have a tendency to warn people of what it is that ails them, hoping to illuminate a new path."

"Not me," I interrupt. "I don't think anyone's life can be changed. The path is set, right?"

Red frowns. "It's a bit much to discuss, don't you think? If we can change what we see? Is that what you're asking?"

"Yes."

"I wish I had a good answer for you, Tydomin. But there isn't a straight one. Let me just say this as a starting point: sometimes we don't grasp what it is that we see. Sometimes we don't understand the full ramifications of the future. We see the *what* of what will happen, but we lack the ability to see *why*."

"What do you mean?"

"I'm sure you've noticed. You might see someone in your life and not know why they are there. You saw me, for example. And though you knew you were to live with me, you couldn't have guessed if this was agreeable or if it was a kidnapping."

The word strikes me hard. "But all that I've seen suggests that I am a willing participant."

"Yes, Tydomin. You can read some of the circumstances, but seers often do things willingly just because they see that they will, in fact, do them. It's a slippery ground."

113

"Try another example, Red. One that isn't scary."

Red looks at me half shocked. "Tydomin," he says, "I didn't mean to suggest that there is anything—"

"I understand," I say. "But you bring to light a point that is a little close to home for what I've been through."

"Okay," he says. "I might see a beautiful woman in my future. I might see that the two of us will be spending a lot of time together; living together, even. I would assume that the two of us are going to be in love. In this assumption, I might pass opportunities to date other women, knowing my destiny lies with another.

"But. In actuality, this woman ends up being a co-worker. We simply work long and hard days on a shared project. Or even worse, it is a poor relationship that I continue to salvage just to keep true to the visions I've seen. It is easy for us to be wrapped up in the wrong assumptions, don't you agree?"

"Did this happen to you?" I ask.

"What?"

"This woman? Is it true for you?"

"Can't you feel it?"

"I haven't tried. I just feel weird about it."

"But do you understand the illustration I gave you?"

"I don't like boys, Red. I'm not worried."

"But you might find yourself asking this," he says. "Why did you let your parents walk out that door?"

"I don't want to talk about it," I say as sharply as I can. I turn away from him to look out the window and see the valley below us. Fog still covers Ashlan, giving the impression that we're driving above the clouds.

"I'm sorry, Tydomin," he says.

"I know," I say. "That's how seers talk to each other, right? Like everything is observed from a distance?"

"Yes."

"Well I have regrets, Red. You knew well enough where to find me so why didn't you stop them from dying?"

"Tydomin," he's speaking softly. "Had I saved them, I would never have known that they were going to die. We are not super heroes."

"So," I still look at the valley covered in fog below. "We can't change anything. We can't save people. What's the point?"

"Like I said. It's complicated. We can't change the big picture, at least not reliably. But don't let that make you think we have no choices. We don't have choices to make and that affects how we live within the context of that big picture.

"No, Tydomin. You cannot blame yourself for what happened to your parents. But that does not absolve you from the ramifications of your decisions. It is our collective decisions that we see, and we have to trust them. We have to trust the decisions that we will make. We are as human as anyone."

"Are we almost there?" I ask, frustration in my voice.

"Yes, Tydomin. Almost."

Martin Oaks

November 18, 2006

I close the door behind Abigail and listen to her go down the steps in the hall. Then I turn around. So I was right. I was right about whom it was that the priest had seen. And according to what Abigail thinks, she works just up the street on Olive.

The room is pitch dark for me without anyone in it. I turn off the lights anyway, to save on the bill. I sit on a pile of cushions by the window and listen to the noise coming from the bar downstairs. This was a big night, talking to Abigail. And Brian is paying me a fortune for my work with her. I try not to think much about it, still. And I try not to think about what to do with the information about Tydomin.

In order to do these things, to not worry about any of it, I have to stop listening with my ears. I focus my attention downstairs and walk in and out of the minds of the people at the bar. I see their depravity and listen to their pathetic concerns.

I feel much better.

Red Scabergrade

December 23, 1997

My house is pretty extraordinary. I spent a good deal of money making a place where I would be comfortable to hardly ever leave throughout my retirement. It's as conspicuous as imaginable, but very few people will ever come down the road which leads to it, and it's nearly half a mile off of the main road past the gate. It's nestled inside a pine forest that runs into the Sequoia National Forest. It sits 6,000 feet above sea level, about 5,700 feet above Ashlan in the valley below.

I stop my truck at the gate and get out to open it. The brisk mountain air smells like pines and the snow, packed tight on the ground, almost squeaks under my boots. I don't like the idea of having a big fancy looking gate that will draw attention from the main road. This one looks old but it's very strong and locked in two places. I leave it unlocked when I know visitors are coming.

After unlocking the gate, I turn to go back to the car. Tydomin is sitting in the passenger seat, still clutching her rabbit, and still looking out the window refusing to talk to me. Her fingers play with the glass on the window, as if she were a child half her age trying to reach a toy incontinently stuck in a television commercial. Her only real efforts are put into not looking at me when I sit down in my seat, springing the bench down under her. This is an understandable reaction in my mind and we both know that she'll start talking to me when we get up to the house.

When I built the house, I had Tydomin in mind. I wanted it to be exciting for her, but made the interior of the side where Tydomin's bedroom is cozy friendly. It's on the opposite side of the house from my bedroom, which I hope will give her a sense of privacy and safety. It's the kind of house that you see in period movies about England in the early 20th century, servants filling the inner organs of the home while the masters plan outings and take teas. It's nestled carefully into the surrounding trees, with a natural drop-off to one side that reveals the town in the valley below framed by treetops.

We pull up to the house and I hear Tydomin say, "Wow," to herself. From the exterior, the house appears to be maybe three stories tall, but really it's just that both floors have very high ceilings. On the front, there are four columns that go from the ground up to the roof. There are not too many windows in the front, but that is compensated by the rear of the house, floor to ceiling glass Overlooking trees and valley.

"Do you like it?"

"Of course."

I stop the car in front of the house, where it will be easier to take in her bags. "Have you seen this house before."

"Yes. I saw it last week. I drew some pictures of the outside. The back is all window?"

"Yes."

"It's really wonderful, Red." I cannot detect any anger in her voice. She seems only happy to be here. I consider for the moment that perhaps the girl wasn't lost in anger at me, so much as lost in her past. I have known feelers who told me that when they are young, then have a very hard time placing themselves in the present except when something very exciting brings them here. It is very similar to what seers go through, not seeing the significance of the present moment as it is such a very small step forward.

Then again, why shouldn't she be angry? It's very hard for me to remember things like the emotional relevance of events, since I spend a lot of time looking ahead as well.

"Here," she says and climbs into the bed of the truck. "Look at this." She digs into a bag that she brought along and produces a sheet of paper. She holds it out to me and I take it.

"This is wonderful, Tydomin," I say looking at the paper. It is a crayon drawing of my house. Not only is it strikingly accurate, but it is also of a very high degree of artistic accomplishment for a child of her age. Well, it's a high degree of accomplishment when compared with what I could do. "When did you draw this?"

"Last night," she says. "I first had glimpses of it last week, but last night I could see it so clearly that I couldn't help but to draw it. They gave me the colors and the paper that I needed."

"Does the drawing *help* you to see it?" I think of how I used to make a habit of journaling what it is I would see, and as the words spilled onto the page, more and more details materialized in my mind.

"I don't know. I suppose so, yes."

I lead her into the house and, to be honest, I take a deal of pride in watching her face light up as we walk in. The living room is majestic with its view out onto the forest. She looked at it with her mouth agape. Then she ran to the center of the room and looked at the piano.

"Look at this," she said. "I saw this last night. It is

so beautiful and exciting. Can you play?"

"I'm afraid not very well and certainly not right now."

"Let's see more," she says as she runs to the doorway, still clutching her rabbit. "My room is this way?"

"Yes," I say. "But slow down. Let's just take our time."

The little girl has a fire in her eyes to see the rest of the house. I feel like she is discovering one of the pleasant truths about seeing; no matter how many times you see something or in how much detail, you never really know what it is going to be like until you're there. That is at least true for those who have a good ability at placing themselves in the present. This looks like a very positive thing in this girl's life.

"Tydomin, you seem very excited," I tell her while she rushes down the hallway to her room. "Can you tell me why?"

"It's just that I haven't seen anything really *new* in so long. I've been doing school at home and staying at home almost every day. When I started seeing all of this, it was strange and confusing, but I wanted to know what it was like. And now, oh my gosh, here it is and here we are and it's all so *different*."

"It is at least that," I say. She rushes up the stairs

and only stops briefly to look out the window at the top of the hall and see the view of the surrounding mountains. I somehow feel bad for the girl in her happiness. To be happy to have something new at the expense of having everything from your old life gone is a heavy trade. Her whole life has been burned to the ground, and all she has in its place is this house. The poor girl cannot see how sad that is right now. Or she chooses not to for the moment.

"My room is up here," she announces to me as if I may not know. She runs into the room and leaps onto the bed. It is a queen-sized four poster bed, all white with a white canopy on top. The room is full of lacy frills, the very catalogue of a girl's room.

"Oh, Red, it's a wonderful room." She looks out at the treetops outside her window. "And what a great window." The sun is setting outside and the snow-covered trees are painted red and pink. As she looks outside, I can see in her eyes that she realizes what a shift this is; that she is something new now. She is quiet and calm for the first time since we stopped the car. Then, her eyes blink and she snaps her head out of it.

"You wanna see something great?" She says to me.

"So now you're showing me around?"

"Yeah. I can't even believe what's next." Again she takes to her heels and rushes out her bedroom door. She dives into a closed door down the hall. "Oh, Red, look at this stuff!"

It is her art room. The room is full of canvases, paints, two different kinds of easels, clay, pallets, and everything else I could buy at the art store.

"How did you know? I mean, I know how you would know, but *why*?"

"Tydomin, you have a real talent for art. I want to make sure that you have every chance to nurture that. You can have lessons in anything you like, and if there is anything missing from this collection, just let me know."

"But it's so much. All I could ever get before was crayons."

"There was a flaw in how you were raised, Tydomin. I'm certain that most of your life revolved around your abilities and that those abilities were seen as a hindrance or curiosity at best. Dwelling on it so much is only going to further make your life revolve around it. While we have a lot to work on in regard to all that stuff, I don't want that to be the only part of yourself that you know. I want you to see other parts of yourself and of life.

"It was a flaw with how I was brought up,

Tydomin. Once my father knew about my ability to see the future, it's all I was ever allowed to do. And all I ever wanted was to play the piano like he did."

She sits down on a padded seat next to an easel. "Tell me more," she says.

I shake my head. "It's not time for that. I don't want to tell you much about my past because someday you will tell me all about it."

"I don't know why, Red, but I don't want to see you with the feeling vision right now."

"All in good time, Tydomin."

Abigail Winters

November 23, 2006

It is my fourth date with Brian. He comes into Stone's for about the last two hours of my shift and orders drinks while he waits for me to get off. I think it's very sweet, but I honestly don't know about someone who sits in a bar by himself without a book or a newspaper or something by his side. I feel just a little bit like I am being watched.

It doesn't help the feeling when he starts asking me about other customers. Last night I waited on a table of three guys who got pretty smashed. One of them started complaining about everything I did, and sent the food back several times. He was loud about the whole thing, too, and seemed to get some kind of pleasure out of kicking me around. I don't like being treated that way or anything, but I'm good at letting it go. I'm good at thinking, "okay, this is just some asshole who is going to leave the restaurant really soon. Blink your eyes and he'll be out of your life, so just endure it."

When I went over to Brian's table to see if I could get him anything, he grabbed my wrist and pulled me down close to him. "What the fuck is that guy's problem?" he said to me just a little too loudly.

"Oh, I know, right? What a jerk."

"You're goddamn right he's a jerk-off. He'd better watch his step." This whole time, he still had his hand holding my wrist a little too tightly.

"Come on, Brian. I'm used to bitchy customers. You learn to let it go." As I said the last part, I jerked my hand free. "Just chill."

"He'd better chill. You shouldn't let him talk to you that way."

"You're not my dad, Brian."

He slammed his drink down on the table and stormed out the door. I felt like he was being a total ass. But then, when I got off of work, he was waiting next to my car with a big bunch of flowers. I ended up being kind of happy that he lost his temper because it gave him a chance to show what a romantic he is. I mean, he was probably just having a bad day or whatever. He wouldn't have gotten flowers for me if he was always such a jerk, or if he was always losing his temper. It was obvious that it was an out of character thing and that he wanted to make it up to me.

He waited for me again tonight, sitting in his corner table. I don't ever stay all the way till closing, but it's pretty late when I get off. It's nice to have someone there who wants to do something. Derek is always in bed by then since he has school the next day. So it's really nice. I haven't kissed the guy or anything and I was just wondering as I was getting off of work if that's the way things are headed. It doesn't have to be, but it's been a long time since I've kissed a guy. The thought sounds kind of nice.

He's leaning against my small truck as I walk out into the parking lot carrying my black apron over my arm.

"Hey beautiful," he says when I get there. And suddenly, ta-da, there we are kissing. It's a pretty aggressive kiss, but that's okay with me. I figure having him wait till the fourth date is at least not slutty of me. But the kiss is a bit, well, toothy for me. He's a macho guy, Brian, and I guess he'll need me to teach him a little bit about how a girl wants to be kissed. There's time for that, I suppose.

"Hi there yourself," I say when our kiss has ended. He's holding me closely to him and I look up, wrapped in his powerful arms.

"Let's go somewhere," he says smiling.

I pull back and give him a confused look. "Where?

Most places are getting pretty close to closing, except the whole bar scene."

"I know a place."

"What kind of place?"

"A good kind."

"Where?"

"Down on Hollywood."

"Yeah, that sounds like a good place. Seriously, where?"

"On Hollywood, seriously. You drive."

He doesn't talk much in the car except to guide me to a little bar downtown where they don't card at the door. They also don't enforce the no-smoking ban that Ashlan has had in effect for several years. That I don't mind so much; it's nice to be able to smoke inside without having to endure the biting cold of winter. But I have forgotten just how much smoke fills a room and creates a haze that's hard to see through. I smoke Cloves, which is kind of a girly flavor, I guess. I look around and notice that I'm one of the few girls around in the place, besides the bartender.

There's a band playing on a small stage. Their music is too loud, but I think that I recognize the drummer. I'm pretty sure it's the guy who used to drum for The Discounted, Vic's old band.

"What are you looking at?" Brian screams over

the music.

"That drummer. Do you know him?"

"No. Why do you care?"

"I think he was Vic's drummer. You remember Vic Neely?"

At the mention of the name, the smile on Brian's face goes down and he sits back. "Yeah. The Discounted, right?"

"Yeah."

"You dated him or something, right?"

"No," I said. "Not really. Or maybe. I'm not sure." I keep to myself how badly I *wanted* to date Vic. I keep to myself that Vic's rejection of me caused the biggest crisis of my life. How I turned to Erica for support and how we almost became more than friends. I keep all of this to myself because the thought of Vic shoves Brian into a shadow. It makes me wonder what I'm doing in a place like this with a guy like this.

"You want something to drink?"

"Diet coke," I say.

He gets up and walks over to the bar. I look back to the band and examine the drummer. I'm sure it's him. It's Dave Wright. I haven't seen the guy since the last time I saw Vic's band play. After a set, I used to sit with Vic and talk about his songs. He trusted my opinions about his music since I was a song writer myself. Sometimes Dave would sit around, too. And whenever Vic disagreed with me about the way I saw a song of his going, one that he was trying out for the first time, Dave would take my side with things. It felt good to be validated in front of Vic, since he could be such a pompous ass about music.

Brian takes a long time to order our drinks, and from the looks of things, the bartender is having a pretty good time with him. She's smiling and laughing and doing that irritating throw-your-head-back-to-smile-and-laugh thing just to show how smitten she is with whatever it is he's saying. I'm not jealous or anything, but it seems kind of rude for him to be flirting on a date that he dragged me to in the first place with his too-toothy kiss.

Brian comes back to our booth just as the band starts to play their next number. Again, the song is too loud so I can't hear the words or even the articulation of the chords. This is what passes for music in most of the local bar scene. This is why I stopped making the rounds and just landed my little act at the Andante. Honestly, though, I don't know how much that's going to last since I really should open up my Sunday availability.

Brian smiles and sits down. I take a sip and almost spit it out. "What the hell?" I say. "It tastes like she spilled sun tan lotion in it."

"It's the Malibu."

"The what?"

"You wanted Diet Coke and Malibu, right?"

"I wanted Diet Coke, anyway."

"I thought the Malibu was implied. Why the hell would you have just a Diet Coke? That's not what you drink on a date."

"It's what I drink on a date. You know, I'm not exactly drinking age, Brian."

"You mean to tell me that you don't drink?"

"No, not really. Not in public and not on a date with a guy who I just started dating. No."

"Whatever," he says and shrugs. He's sipping on some kind of a light colored beer and is grooving his head bobs to wherever he supposes the beat is to the song that's too loud. I notice that he doesn't offer to get up and get me another drink, one that I might actually want to, you know, drink.

This isn't really my idea of a date, I come to realize. This isn't a lot of fun, sitting in a room full of smoke and music that's deafening and a drink that I didn't order on a night when I'm pretty fucking tired and want to go to bed. Out of kindness to Brian, who I still believe to be a pretty good guy, I just sit here the rest of the night and bob my head to wherever I suppcse to beat of the song is supposed to be.

On the way out of the bar, finally at 2 am, I make eye contact with Dave. He did a quick double-take, then smiled and gave me the "what's up" head jerking thing. Then he sort of squinted his eyes at Brian, like he was either trying to recognize him or he was trying to figure out why the two of us were hangirg out.

I was glad to have driven because it meant that I got to drive home. In the car, I can smell the alcohol on Brian's breath and his words are a little slurred. He must have had four beers, but I didn't exactly sit there and count so it could have been more or less.

Finally, as we're getting back towards Mission Square, he says, "So, you want to come over to my place or what?"

"No, thanks, Brian."

"C'mon. Why not?"

"You're drunk for one. For another, I have to get to bed. I'm dead tired."

"I have to get to bed, too." He's smiles this smile and leans over like he's so fucking clever and I'm going to laugh my way into his pants.

"Thanks, I like my bed."

"Well I don't have a problem with going back to your place," he says.

By now we're parked at his car, the last one sitting in the Stone's parking lot. "Good night, Brian."

"You expect me to drive?"

"Damn," I say to myself. I can't let him drive, but I don't want to sit here and continue to turn him down for another three miles or whatever, but I do.

Derek Neely

November 18, 2006

Ashlan is not an old town by most any standards. But as far as neighborhoods go, the ones surrounding Mission Square tend to be very nice, well established neighborhoods, as they say. Most of the houses are older, all of them are large, and a good percentage of them are just plain opulent. Some of the houses, the really big ones, are newer and built on the graves of the homes that used to occupy their lot. These houses, no doubt, were nearly expensive looking enough for the rich owners.

The trees in these neighborhoods are beautiful. They're much older than the ones in many of the other neighborhoods or areas of town. All of the central valley, pretty much, is treed simply because people planted non-native trees, but at least the ones here have been here long enough to grow to some measure of majesty. Up high you have the eucalyptus, oak, and ash trees; down low there are Japanese maples and citrus trees.

It's in one of these neighborhoods, clouded in fog, where Tydomin and I are walking. I footsteps sound loud in the silence, beating out a measure of time on the concrete sidewalk. Our hands are thrust firmly in our pockets against the cold air.

"So you grew up here?" Tydomin asks.

Questions like this one are hard to answer for me. Yeah, I grew up here, so? It just doesn't really arm her, ultimately, with any kind of information that let's her know the slightest thing about me. I mean, after all, I just don't consider myself too much like anyone else who grew up here. "Yeah," I answer and leave it at that. All the complication is smoothed out with a simple one-word answer that lets her start to assume whatever it is she assumes about people who grew up here. "How about you?"

"I was born here," Tydomin says. "But I did a lot of my growing up in the mountains."

"Your parents live up there still?"

"My parents died," she says as if that is something that you say, kind of like observing that the sun is going down.

"I'm sorry," I say lamely.

"I know. I know that everyone is sorry that my parents died. Live with it; I do."

"So who did you live with up in the mountains?"

"My guardian. I think of him as a father a lot of the time. I called him that on good days. Other days, he was just Red."

We're quiet for a while, merely walking. I did exactly what I was afraid I was going to do. I walked right into her most horrifying childhood fact, uncovered it, put it out on the table, and now we're sitting in the face of it sorry we both were born. I tend to do this every single time I talk to a girl. There was a girl in my Anatomy class who I jokingly asked if she came from a long line of retards. Well, damn it, she did.

"See this house," Tydomin says out of the blue. She walks up towards one of the larger houses and starts stepping on the lawn. I look around to make sure no security guards are coming to tackle us. "This is a lot like the house I grew up in."

The house is large and white. It has some kind of Corinthian columns going up the front, reaching up two or three floors to the roof. It reminds me of some kind of plantation home you see depicted in movies about small towns in Georgia that always make you think you want to visit Georgia when, in fact, you do not want to visit Georgia.

"It's beautiful."

"Yes," she says. "Mine was better. It had wings going out to either side, one for me, one for Red." She turns and looks at me. "He's the man who raised me from the time I was seven."

I nod.

"It was a beautiful place. But so imposing, you know? Just crouched there in the woods, like it grew up out of the ground along with all of the trees, or was unearthed with the rocks. It was its own little universe. It had the most beautiful piano in it."

I chuckle to myself. "I've never heard anyone ever describe a childhood home as 'imposing.' And you keep talking about it like it's gone."

"It is," she says. "It burned down last year."

"Damn," I say. Again, that ability to walk right into the fire in conversations makes itself so apparent. "What happened?"

"You don't want to know."

"I'm going to have to disagree with you. I do, indeed, want to know why your house burned down."

"It was complicated," she says. "We'll talk about it some time. It's a long story."

"It's a long night."

"Not long enough."

We walk on, leaving the imposing house behind

us. I notice that she's constantly breathing air into her cupped hands. "Hey," I say. "Do you want to borrow my gloves?"

"You have gloves?"

"Yeah, I wasn't really wearing them," I say. "I felt bad wearing gloves when you're obviously so cold. Then, just now, I made the connection that we both didn't need to be deprived of warm hands. So why not offer them, right? Better late than never."

Her smile shines. It's like whenever I say or do something that makes her happy, she's about a zillion times happier that I would think she would be. Don't get me wrong, it's totally validating. I capture her smile in my mind because tonight, while I'm sitting alone in my house, I'm going to want to go over every moment of this whole evening, I know. And I'll want proof that she's interested in me, proof that she's not just killing time or jerking me around, proof that she would like to see me again and that I won't be imposing on her to ask her out next time I come in to the bookstore. This smile, lit in the foggy darkness by a distant street light and too-soon Christmas lights on a too-big house, will be all the proof I'm looking for. Her shining face, right now, though it lasts for only a few decaying seconds, will keep me happy for days, I can tell.

"Thank you so much," she says. "You have no

idea how nice that is."

"I do, actually. It's really nice. And your smile tells me that." And now, wow, I thought the smile was good. I thought I was going to snap that picture of her smile and live on it, but man, this is better. This is something that I can not only live on, but thrive on. She blushes. She blushes like a shy girl in an old movie. It makes me aware of myself, makes me see us standing there from an outside perspective and say from a detached and subjective point of view, *Wow, that guy has that girl enchanted.*

But, honestly, it's all her. And on some level it feels like a joke. How can I like someone this much and have her like me back?

We walk a while, now holding hands, and I keep wondering what it is that I've done. Did hanging around like a stalker really succeed in turning this girl on?

We walk a circle in the neighborhood and come back to Mission Square. We walk into the mission itself and sit down on a bench under an over hang. It's colder staying still, but we look out at Olive Street and sit close, enjoying each other's warmth.

The mission here is really somewhat of an oddity. California has tons of Spanish missions going up and down the coast, each one built like a day's walk or something away from each other so that Indians could be properly converted even while traveling up the coast. How cozy; evenly spaced slave camps masked in salvation.

At some point, so my fifth grade California History class would have me believe, they wanted to make a road connecting the mountains to the coast in order to get at the Indians who lived in the mountains in the rumored valleys that the Spaniards had heard of from other Indians. They started by building this one, about half way between the two worlds. Supposedly, the missionaries got here at a particularly wet part of a particularly wet year and they assumed that the San Joaquin River was a thriving river with all kinds of potential for shipping things all over the state.

Come the summer, the river dried up to its normal trickle and the valley was scorched by unbearable heat. The missionaries realized the miracle of irrigation they were going to have to daily perform to get any kind of crops going. They abandoned the mission before it was quite completed and went back to work in areas that showed more potential. Years later, as the area became settled, the Catholic Church moved back into the land it had claimed before and completed the mission. Here it stands now, a monument to poor planning and the power of a settled population.

"This is a beautiful town," Tydomin says.

"Ashlan?"

"Yeah."

"Now I get it," I say, relieved as if a steam-valve had opened up releasing tension. "You're crazy. I've been sitting here all night wondering what it is that you see in me, and now I can see what it is. You're a total nut-job."

"Stop it," she says, half annoyed. "I'm not crazy."

"Blind?"

"I'm far from bind, Derek."

"I've spent my entire childhood dreaming of escaping this place, moving on to some place that *matters* a little bit more."

"I've dreamed of leaving it, too, Derek. It's just that right now, I feel like I can see it for what it is, just a little bit more. It's one of those moments when the trees in the forest come into focus, and you see how pretty it is; it's not just a tangle of woods, but a collection of individual trees."

We sit and look out at the lights, shining through their halos. "So what is it that you do, Tydomin?" I ask at last.

"What do you mean?"

sight

"You're a home schooled high school girl who works at a bookstore. There's got to be something else. What moves you? What do you do?"

"Are you hoping I'm a musician?"

"No. I've had plenty of them in my life."

"Good," she says. "I'm an artist."

"Really?"

"Yeah. I'll show you some of my stuff sometime. Actually, I have two pieces hanging in the bookstore right now."

I move back mentally in my head. I look at the map of the bookstore that I have memorized so well in my tenure as a book clerk stalker. "Not the landscape of the trees with the snow?" I say.

"Yes, that's one."

"No way."

"Why do you say that?"

"Because it's insanely beautiful," I say. "I figured it was a copy ordered from some MOMA collection. There is such a structure to that painting, like the emotional qualities come across in the brush strokes."

"What emotional qualities?"

I think about this for a second, trying to conjure the painting in my head. On the nights that I wandered the shelves, I often stopped at that painting to get lost in something other than books. "To me that painting says something about searching. It's like you're traveling somewhere in that painting, looking at these trees deep in a forest and you realize that wherever you're going, you're a damn far way away. But there's something welcoming about where you are."

"Yes?"

"And you just can't stay there. It's not for you, you know? It's like a moment in a road trip or something when you realize how far away from home you are, and how you're not close to where you're going, but it's pretty and for a minute you stop your rush and you stop your running." I find myself thinking, all of a sudden, of a particular morning in southern New Mexico when I was younger. My brother and I woke up early—accidentally—and watched the sun light up the surrounding mountains. And for a minute, we wished we weren't headed to Houston.

She shakes her head. "I never saw that. You're making that up."

"No," I say. "I swear to God. I always look at that painting and I see a wandering soul, like how John Muir would just pick up and head out by himself and see what he could find, never happy with where he was. That's what that painting says."

She looks at me, again with some kind of

shininess. I snap a picture in my head. I can't wait to develop these images when I get home, to bask in the glory of what was my best night where no matter how hard I tried, I just couldn't seem to ruin everything.

***

Forgive this intrusion. There's something happening here that none of these characters are seeing properly that has to be brought to the fore. There are dots to be connected across time and lives (that you've probably already guessed by now) that even the brightest of these characters cannot realize enough to comment upon from their lonely perspectives. These things are hidden in the shadows from them and deserve some modicum of illumination. This intersection of characters is mostly all rested on one single event (that has yet to transpire in these pages) that may seem somewhat inconsequential. But the effects resonate in the moods of these characters, in their actions, in their lives, and in this small spark of something between these two youngest of the cast. I'm putting a signpost here, rooting it in the middle of these pages, hoping to give the discerning reader a bit of a lens that our cast just doesn't have.

The first time Tydomin saw Vic, it was associated with Red's client, Alan. And it was in a vision of the future. To be perfectly accurate, it was also the first time she saw Derek, though she never really made that connection until much later.

She didn't see Vic so much as a living, breathing person who seemed to gather people around him with his enthusiasm but was actually shrouding his own inability to accomplish what he wanted in life; that's just how she came to see him after several private and very candid conversations. No, that first time she saw him as a statistic, as fallout, as collateral damage. He was the second person that would die as a result of a mistake that she made, and in her young mind at the time, the less important of those two people. Derek was just the guy who was with the guy who died in her vision, nameless, faceless, pointless accessory to the story that she had unknowingly unfolded.

You see, it was Tydomin's personal struggle with her own biological abnormality (spiritual abnormality, perhaps?) that ended up driving so much of Derek's life and Vic's death. And it was entirely unintended.

For most of us, there is no knowing how many small decisions we make may harm other people. For most of us, if we stop for coffee on the way to wherever it is we are going and that somehow leads to someone else's pain, suffering, or death, we are in the dark about things. We don't see the dominoes fall, from small, menial decisions. And while this is something she was so able to accept even when her own parents died, it wasn't so easy in this case. It was a biological reaction, really, that let her let her parents die. There's any number of things she could have done to save them, such as lighting the house on fire before they were to go out that night. It wasn't so easy for her, and the reason it wasn't is so locked up in her being, that she must surely not be aware of it. The same sort of force that would drive you or me to draw a breath after a certain amount of time underwater— even though it would be the beginning of the end— made her adhere to the world she had foreseen. How could she foresee it, if it wasn't to happen, biologically speaking?

But Vic's death was something else. It was a direct result of an actual *decision* she had made. A decision to fight her biology and make a small change in her life that resulted in an entire revision of the future for many people. Her decision isn't one of will, like it would be for you (presumably, of course) or me, but a decision of the body, of the blood, and of her heritage. And so, then little, tiny changes of minds that trickled through other decisions that ended up catastrophic for one single person and those people that he knew.

That first time, though, she wasn't all broken up about it. Not about *him* anyway. It wasn't until she saw him *in the flesh* for the first time, and found out that those who she knew, including the girl she was living with, were going to be touched so heavily by his death that she felt that pang of regret. It was then that she tried to reverse the damage that had already been done.

chapter 6

Tydomin White

February 10, 1998

Living with Red is getting better. He makes sure I do my schoolwork still, which isn't my favorite, but he lets me skip ahead to things that are more interesting. He doesn't follow the curriculum that Ashlan School District supplies us with. Instead I'm allowed to go ahead and get to the exciting things.

But the best part by far is the art supplies. I have this big textbook with art supplies in it. I point and he finds me what I need.

I paint. And I mean I paint every day here. On real canvasses. When he saw just how excited I got about painting, he ran out and got me several books about the old masters. We study them together. And I study technique books and I spend almost every morning painting for an hour or so before breakfast. I feel proud of what I paint, but I wouldn't say that they're really good. I think a regular girl my age would probably say so, but I've spent so much time looking at the real art in these books, and I've also spent time looking at my own art in the future.

Just like Red said, I can't tell how the art is going to make me *feel*, and that's really bothering me. But I can see the paintings and I can see that I'm going to be very good in just a few more years. Painting seems to be my thing, for the years that I can see, anyway. I don't have a lot of interest in sculpture or woodwork or anything else like mixed media or anything. I just like painting because it's so vibrant and colorful. It's so wonderful to see part of the world turned flat, and in doing so, making it understandable and meaningful.

I'm getting better at painting, and I'm getting better at mixing paints. I try and picture the exact shade and color that I want and I try and make exactly that mix. I'm pretty good at getting the colors to run into each other without any seams. It doesn't hurt that the paints that Red got me are like the best paints you can buy.

I'm also getting better at the whole *seeing* thing, too. I haven't been here that long, really, but Red has worked with me on it. I think it helps just being around someone who believes me. But not only does he believe me, we also has stories to tell me about it. And he shows me how he sees things, too. We talk about it like it's normal stuff, like it's homework or the dishes or going to the store or something. And I feel really *normal* about it. Even though I know it's not normal.

Red told me that there are lots of kids who are born the way we are who never find out. Either they never nurture it and the ability goes away, or they nurture it above other things in their lives and they kind of lose their minds. It seems unlikely to me that I could lose my mind just looking into the future; it's like if you said that you're afraid that you're going to take flight just by running. It might be a complication, and it does seem kind of unpleasant to see the future, but I'd never lose my mind over it.

I asked him how he knew that there were kids born like we are who never find out. If they never find out, I'm sure they don't tell anyone anything about it or anything like that, so how do you know? Red was calm and cool , like he normally is, and he told me that if I knew half the things he knew about "how *They* studied these children and found out what they were capable of," I'd be more thankful about what he was trying to do for me.

That got me to thinking about his past again. I never have sat and looked at his past. I've looked at his future a dozen times and I can tell you that it's pretty boring from what I actually see. But he has me do a detailed viewpoint, as we call it, just about what I'm going to see the next day. I write it out, then—and this is my addition—I draw a picture from something that am going to see the next day. It's kind of tedious, like doing the dishes or something. But the drawing part is a lot of fun, as long as I can see something interesting to draw. It's snowy up here right now and I spend some time on the balcony looking out at the pines all covered in white and listening to the quietness that the snow lays on the world. I end up drawing some of that on a lot of nights.

A couple times a month, Red and I go down the mountain into Ashlan or Selma. We do some shopping and run some other errands. Twice we've checked in with the social worker ladies and talked about how things are going and what adjustments are like and that kind of stuff. It's always hard because pretty soon I start thinking about things again and everything seems so impossible.

There are other times when I don't even know that Mom and Dad are gone. Red says it's because of my feeling abilities. I can get lost in them, he says, and I don't even know what's real or what's now or what's what. And sometimes, I've noticed, I'm not sure if I've living the day or looking at it from behind or from past the day. I guess this really used to happen to me all the time, but since I've been talking about it with Red so much, I'm able to notice those days when I'm not sure how it fits into the timeline of things. That must sound really confusing.

Red said that for seers, urgency has to be learned. We're infinitely patient, he says, and I've noticed that. I never did know why other kids would be so excited about birthdays or holidays or even days off from school. Back when I went to school, before all the trouble I started, I didn't really understand what was so great about a Saturday that couldn't be watched on a Thursday. So I could shuffle my feet through the day and just watch the time off I was going to have, or the presents I was going to open if my birthday was coming up. And I was never really sad about going to school because, after all, there I was living whatever day from my past I wanted to.

This is a problem for a lot of seers and feelers, Red tells me. So we work a lot on separating them with these little busy exercises. If I can't quite place myself in my actual time, people can take advantage of me, he tells me. While I can't really tell how well the exercises work, he says that I probably won't knowingly see the difference for a really long time, since things are so mixed up inside me and I'll remember things to be more clearly than they actually were.

One of the things he has me do is sit and watch a candle. I watch the flame flicker and I use my seeing vision to watch what the flame is going to do, then I instantly watch it do it. This is a quick way to see the way that our present interacts with the future. The changes in a candle are so quick that I don't have to wait and see things in the present. The other idea about this exercise is to get bored. I don't get bored really easily because it's so easy to see something else or feel something else from some other time. But since I'm busy doing something over and over and over again, and it's so connected to the *now,* I do get bored.

While boredom is bad, it's good to have some kind of feeling attached to the present. It's rare for me, too. It really reminds me that, hey, I'm here right now. And Red says that the feeling can be remembered and should be constantly called back anytime I feel like I'm drifting into another time.

Maybe then I could go to school again.

Today, Red is making me do homework. He has this huge packet of materials he got from the schools that I have to go over. And even though he goes easy and lets me move ahead and stay behind in things, I still have a lot of work to do. Red says that I'm going to move very fast and be ahead of everyone when I get to high school age. I told him that I want to go to school and maybe then I could start and everything would be easy for me. Even though he knows if I'll do that or not, he didn't say. But he said that I have to trust whatever decision I make, once I can see it, because it's probably the wisest one.

Later, Red has a meeting. Some man is coming and they're going to go into Red's office and close the door. Red hasn't talked about this man or this meeting at all, and from what I can see, he isn't going to talk about it afterwards. I don't know what's so secret about it. I don't think that I'll even see the man; I'll just hear him come in and hear him leave. I keep thinking that this might be a good chance to see if I can change the things I see and sneak around and catch a glimpse of him. Something tells me I won't, though.

sol smith

Red Scabergrade

February 10, 1998

"We are having a visitor today," Tydomin suddenly says at breakfast. "Why don't you want me to meet him?"

"What makes you think I don't want you to meet him?"

The girl rolls eggs around her plate with a fork. "I don't know. I can see that I'm not going to and that just doesn't seem too normal. I don't think that you should keep me here as if it's some kind of secret."

The girl is progressing very well. In just a few short weeks she has come a long way not so much in how far she can see as much as how accurate she is. She sees more clearly and her analysis of what she sees is much more accurate as well. I'm not used to having someone else around yet, much less someone who can see, so I am learning how to avoid these misunderstandings little by little. Disclosure isn't something I'm used to, but I feel that it has to be embraced in order for her

160

not to feel a prisoner of me or of anything else in her life.

"Tydomin, I'm sorry I didn't mention it. We are having a visitor today. And you're right; I don't want you to meet him. As a matter of fact, Tydomin, I do hope to keep you secret from him."

She puts her forks down on the table hard, making it bang against the wood. "Red, I don't think it's right to keep me secret. It makes me feel bad and I don't think it looks really good for you."

"Try and understand, Tydomin. I don't want to keep you secret from *everyone*. But this man especially should never know about you, if we can help it. He is a dangerous man."

She looks at me sideways. "Why are you meeting with a dangerous man?"

"It is part of the life that I hope to spare you from. Most seers, if they adjust to their abilities at all, end up making a living by exploiting their talents. By nature of the facts of these talents, the people who pay for them are dishonest. Many of the people who can afford very big projects are dishonest to a very high level."

Tydomin looks back to her eggs. "Well, I don't think you should do it."

"And why not?"

"Can't you just win the lottery and not need any

money?"

"Yes, I can. Or play the stock market. Or patent an invention or two. Believe me, I have plenty of money."

"Then why do you keep doing jobs?

"Your question is more complicated than you assume. It has a very complicated set of answers. This job, for example, is directly tied to my past. In many ways it would be unavoidable."

"He's someone from your past?"

"No. Like I said, this is all very complicated. But there's something I've done in my past that has to be protected. And this man is going to be instrumental in doing that, though he has no idea of that right now. Likewise, this is directly linked to my future, and yours. I'm hoping that by doing this job—a very dishonest job with a very dangerous character—is going to insure your future. You are a thoughtful and creative girl and, I believe, worth much more than the life that I've led."

Tydomin stands up from the table and clears her plate. "What's so wrong about the life that you've led?"

"Why haven't you taken a look at my past with your abilities?"

"I couldn't begin to tell you," the girl says. "I feel like there's a reason behind it, like I want *you* to tell me. Or maybe it just feels creepy. You know, I never looked much at my parents' pasts because it felt like a bit of an intrusion, I think."

"It's just as well, Tydomin. I don't think that you'd find my past very interesting right now. You may just as well wait. But I do think that we need to work on your feeling skills a little more than we have been."

"Do you think that's something that you can teach me, without being able to feel yourself?"

"I may not be the best, but I have some ideas. I was thinking that we'd take a trip, or a few trips, to places of historical interest. That way you'll be able to work on much more distance than just looking at individual people. Plus, it will work well for your school work."

She rolls her eyes at the thought of school work.

Martin Oaks

November 24, 2006

"I just don't get it," he whines. "I feel like I'm losing her already."

"You kissed her, right?"

"Yeah, a few times."

"Sounds like things are going well to me."

Brian has been my least favorite client for a while. But as is always true of my least favorite clients, he is loaded. I mean loaded. His single-mom left him with his grandfather when he was about five and never came back. Later, it turned out there was a trust fund set up for him by his biological father as some sort of substitute for fathering. The fund matured quite a bit. Not fully trusting the kid, his grandfather kept this a secret. It stayed a secret until Brian was 19 and his grandfather died. Then out of the blue, some lawyer shows up and tells him he's a millionaire, after taking his own cut, of course.

It always happens to the absolute jackasses.

I saw him in Stones one day about two months ago. I could tell he was sitting there with money burning on his mind. I walked over and made my pitch; that I was a psychic running a shop upstairs and that I could help him. He laughed, as I expected, and asked what I could help him with.

"That waitress," I said. I could see through Brian's eyes that he hadn't so much as looked at me since I sat down at his table. His eyes were locked on the pretty young girl with long black hair who was waiting tables. I could see the thoughts he was thinking about her, the ways he'd like to have her, what it would mean in terms of ownership to him.

"What do you mean?" And for the first time he looked at me.

"First you have some business to take care of." I looked at him and made eye contact as best I could. "You're in a relationship right now," I said slowly. "But I don't see it lasting. Which is good, of course, because she's not the kind of girl who would run around with someone who's running around, you know?"

"You don't think? Yeah, you're a fucking Eisenstein."

"She's cheating on you. Your girlfriend. I shouldn't be telling you, of course, I'm sure you've figured that our yourself."

His mind reacted more violently than I might have expected. Especially since I could see that he had actually cheated on his girlfriend quite a few times.

"Come upstairs and bring your wallet, if you want to talk about how to remedy this situation."

He was hooked. It only takes that much for a lot of people. Sure, it's really easy when I have people walk into the shop because they're self-selecting; they already are going to believe what I tell them. But being that most of them come for advice on money, they don't have that much to throw my way. I charge them exactly what I think I can to get them to come back in another week or two. But when I can land a big fish like Brian, the trick is to get him to come in as much as possible and still feel like you're not wasting his time and money. You set up a project with him that has several complicated steps to it. You maneuver them around like chess pieces, let each complication get them caught up more, and make it look like they can never finish this project. But steps are still being accomplished in different areas, making the illusion of progress quite real to them.

What looked to Brian like a simple operation— dump his girlfriend, bone the hot young waitress—I made him take two months doing. And, I saw in the waitress' mind that she wasn't interested in bedding the asshole, so that will be another month or so of wrangling. In the mean time, I've taken Brian fully out of his comfort zone, made him start a romantic relationship and promised him that every possible complication was bringing him a step closer—just come back tomorrow night.

Now I have to show him what an asshole he is for taking Abbie to that stupid bar. One or two nights without paying for my advice and he goes and runs back to his comfort zone—get the underage girl lousy drunk and see if she'll sleep with you. Hell, it's worked for him in the past, so why wouldn't he give it a try?

"You've made a big misstep, Brian," I say. "We need to pick up the pieces."

"You know what? Fuck it. Just fuck it. Why do I care about this bitch?"

"Now come on, Brian. You dumped your girl for her. Need I remind you what you did to Caroline in order to get rid of her? The way you went all-out like that to tear things apart and make that poor girl's world crumble down around her? It's not enough for you, Brian, to have just any girl anymore," I say. Appealing to Brian's greed is often more useful than appealing to his lust. "Girls that will go out with any guy with a bunch of money to throw around end up being with a lot of guys. But girls like this don't go for just anyone; so few end up possessing them."

The biggest problem in the whole thing has been Abigail.

Abigail has been a client of mine for six months or so. She's the other kind of client. She scrapes what tips she can together just to get into my shop once a week. She asks general questions and I intuit what answers she wants. I've been selling her this Berkley fantasy for a few weeks now when Brian had finally gotten to the stage of his plan where he wanted to make a move on Abbie.

It sucks. She's a better person than he is. She's humble and though she's not Christian by a long shot, she knows she's a sinner and is constantly aware of the fact that she is a disappointment to the gods whom she used to believe in. She's aware of her dead mother at every turn and always hoping that whatever form her mother is in, she's not watching her because she's fallen so low of expectations. A rocky relationship with her father, no relationship with her mother, she barely finished high school and decided that she just wasn't ready for something like college out of the blue.

I wish she were going to Berkley. I wish she did have some kind of plan in life. But, honestly, I'm the wrong person for her to talk to. And this thing with

Brian won't last, I can just tell. Sooner or later, he will decide that Abigail isn't the girl for him and I'll make him think that was his idea. When the whole thing blows up, I'm guessing I'll lose Abbie as a client, but that's for the better for her. I don't need the $20 a week so badly as she does, anyway.

"Abigail," I tell Brian, "is impressed by gestures of apology. She never had that in her household and those whom she's dated in the past have been pretty rough on her emotionally."

This seems to have gotten his attention. "Who did she date before?"

"Why do you care?"

"You know, don't you? I mean, you can use your powers to see that, right?"

I act like I'm using my powers. It's interesting the ways you can convince someone of something by just spending a little time in their head. "Yes, I can see who she dated."

"A drummer? Did she date some drummer named Dave?"

"Yes," I say. She didn't, as far as I know, as far as the time I've spent in the girl's head, but man does Brian want that to be true. I can't quite figure out why. I think he wants to feel smart.

"I saw her making eyes at the guy last night. I think

she still has something for him."

"To be fair, Brian, I told you not to take her to any bars."

"Yeah, what you told me what wasn't working either."

I smile. "Patience, Brian. This isn't some plan of mine, it's what I have foreseen."

Abigail Winters

December 3, 2006

Brian is getting better at this boyfriend thing. Little by little. He's seems to know the right thing to do or say at the right time. He's so charming and confident. And there's something about his constant screwing up and his constant attempts to make everything better that show me that this is a man who is trying so hard. He's trying to win my affections, and I just don't know what it is that he sees in me so much. But if feels good to be *wanted* for once.

Vic was great. He was a great friend. I really slipped up when I slept with him. One little mistake like that I think it just crushed how I felt about myself. I don't think it was Vic's fault. No, it wasn't Vic's fault that I ended up being hurt. He misread the situation and thought we were just "hooking up." I thought it was more. I thought our friendship, which was in place for so long, had just blossomed.

Vic was used to being wanted. Vic was popular,

exciting, enticing. I was plain.

Now I feel wanted. It feels great. Brian bends over backwards just to please me, and it works a good deal of the time. He knows what movies I like to watch, he knows where I like to shop, and damn if he doesn't stick with me while I shop. He's stopped suggesting that I go out drinking with him anymore and he hasn't taken me back to that godforsaken bar.

Tonight Brian is taking me out to a restaurant. Some kind of fancy restaurant where he swears to God the prime rib will make me want to die. That's cute; the thought that I'm going to go out to some restaurant and order prime rib. Once again I am driving, because he may end up drinking. He has some kind of really good fake I.D. and I told him that it doesn't bother me when he uses it, even though it does a little. He looks old and a lot of times he isn't carded at all. He's so good at acting like he *knows* he's old enough to order drinks.

We walk into the restaurant and he tells the hostess that we're there for our reservation. I can't remember the last time that I ever went to a restaurant with a reservation at all. The place is really nice; one of those places with low light and soft music coming from somewhere you can't see. The waiters all wear black, but with white aprons that just go up to their waists. I'm just giddy about the whole thing.

We sit down and are greeted by our waiter. And I just can't believe me eyes when I see who it is.

"Dave?"

"Hey, Abbie, what have you been up to?" He smiles at us.

"How long have you worked here?"

"Oh, I don't know, just about as long as the place has been open. Was that you downtown a few weeks ago?"

"Hell yeah, that was me," I say and then cover my mouth, thinking about where we are, some kind of nice place where the other customers don't want to hear "hell" thrown around so casually.

"I'm Brian," Brian stands up and gives Dave one of those handshakes where he squeezes the other guy's fingers just so the other guy doesn't have a chance of getting in a firm handshake. "I'm Abigail's boyfriend."

"Good to meet you," Dave says. "I didn't know you were dating anyone," he says to me. "That's great."

Brian sits back down. "I'll have a Guinness. She'll have a Diet Coke."

Dave kind of stops smiling. "Cool, can I see an I.D?"

Brian glares at Dave. "Seriously?"

"Yeah, the manager is really big on carding

everyone."

"I was in here last week and they didn't card me."

"Sorry, bro. I've got to see it."

Brian huffs and reaches into his pocket. He pulls it out and hands the I.D. to Dave. He looks at me with one of those smirks that says, "Can you believe this guy?" But I just smile politely and unfold my stiff napkin.

"I thought you said your name was Brian," Dave says.

"Brian's my middle name. I can't stand Steven."

Dave looks at me and frowns. "I'm sorry," he says more to me. "I can't serve you. Not unless you show me a credit card or something else with Steve written on it."

Brian is seething. "I can't believe that you're giving me this attitude."

"What can I get you to drink?" Dave is not amused.

"Just the Guinness."

"I'm sorry. Is there anything else?" Dave is acting all fancy-waiter, adopting this air of formality that I'm sure goes over in a place like this, especially when trying to gloss over conflicts.

Me, I'm just embarrassed.

Brian slams his fist on the table. "I want to talk to

your manager."

"That's a good idea. Let me go and get him."

Dave walks off and I'm left with Brian. Brian can be such a hot head and I don't think I've ever seen him quite this bad. "Just Chill, Brian," I say. "Have a Pepsi or something."

"Just shut up, Abbie. I'm going to get your ex-boyfriend fired."

I glare at Brian. "He's not my ex."

"Whatever." He snaps this word at me and I can see in his eyes that for whatever reason it's me that he's angry at.

I stand up. "I'm going to the bathroom."

As I walk away, the manager comes to the table and starts to talk to Brian. Brian is talking loudly to the manager and I'm glad to get away before he gets embarrassing. I look at my watch and I can see that we've literally been in here less than five minutes. Five minutes and Brian has gone from charming-guy Brian to total-asshole Brian; it's got to be some kind of a record, even for him.

When I walk out of the bathroom, I can see that the manager is still standing at our table and Brian's arm movements speak to his anger. I decide to just stand in the bar until it blows over. It's so shitty when he's this way, but I remind myself that this just means

175

that later on he'll be extra nice. He can be a real roller-coaster ride.

"So Abbie, what's the deal with your boyfriend?" Dave is standing next to the bar, keeping an eye on our table through the doorway. He doesn't look at me when talking, just keeps his eyes fixed on the manager and my date.

"I don't know," I say. "He can lose his temper pretty easily. He's a good guy, I swear. He needs a little work, a little polishing."

Dave shrugs. "I don't know, Abbie. Didn't he used to date Caroline Rogers?"

"Rings a bell. But I don't care about who he used to date."

"Maybe you should. The rumor was that he hit the girl around."

I look at Dave in disbelief. "No way."

"I've seen the guy down at that hole-in-the-wall on Hollywood just about every night the band plays there."

"You guys sounded great."

He shrugs. "Thanks, but I think we kind of sound like shit. I just want to play. Anyway, I see Brian down there and everyone was talking about how he hit Caroline around all the time. But, you know, she's been in a couple relationships like that. It's like she attracts that kind of treatment somehow, it's some kind of cycle."

"You have to be thinking of someone else."

"I don't know, look at him." And Dave had a point there. Still Brian was yelling at the manager, now standing up shoving a finger in the direction of the waiter. Finally Brian gives up whatever it was he was arguing, like the manager was going to go into the back of the bar and come out with a keg of booze for him now. He marches over to where Dave and I are standing.

"It was good to see you," Dave says and he hugs me.

"It was good to see you, too, Dave," I say. And suddenly Dave is pulled away from me and I'm shoved to the ground.

"What the fuck do you think you're doing?" Brian yells in Dave's face. He's shoving Dave and it looks like he's going to hit him. This nice restaurant, a place of decorum, is transformed into a quiet and uncomfortable backdrop, centered around these two men; Brian, wild-eyed and erect, Dave, leaning lazily against the bar, looking half awake.

"I'm sorry, man," Dave says.

"Stop it," I yell out. I rush to get between the two of them, facing Brian. "Leave him alone and let's get the hell out of here." Now I've become part of the floorshow, I realize—the crazy girl who instigated the whole thing somehow. I hate yelling like this in public. "Stop standing up for your fuck of a boyfriend," Brian yells at me. I turn around and storm out of the restaurant, unwilling to participate in the play anymore. Brian is on my heels, since the manager is walking over saying something about the police that I'm too infuriated to listen to. "Bye, Dave." I call over my shoulder. "It was nice to see you." I manage to avoid the eyes of the customers as I make the unbelievable long twenty-foot walk to the door.

I unlock my truck and get in. Brian is pounding on the passenger side door and I reluctantly reach over and unlock his side.

"What the fuck was that about, Abbie? Why was his dicking with us like that? He wants revenge on you."

"You're full of shit, Brian," I yell. "I never dated him and he wasn't dicking with anyone. You were trying to pass off your stupid I.D. in a nice place and you ruined the whole night."

To that, Brian just sits back in his chair and looks out the window. I hit a nerve. He did ruin the whole night and he knew it. I feel like he had a lot invested in tonight. Again I think that probably his idea was to get me into bed with him. It's not what I want to do. I don't see a big rush and it creeps me out when he has some plan like that. Instead of feeling wanted, I feel dirty and preyed upon.

"I think we should take a little time off," I tell him.

"What?"

"I think that maybe I want to go a week or so without seeing you," I say. "I think it would do both of us some good."

"Fuck it. Whatever."

Derek Neely

December 8, 2006

"You're going to need a heavier coat than that," I tell Tydomin.

"Are you sure?"

"Oh yeah, it's way cold out there and it's way colder in the foothills. You need a big coat and probably a hat."

"You can't keep me warm?"

"I like what you're saying, but it's really cold. Like really."

We hop into my car and I go over everything in my head. I can't think of anything that I forgot, which just means that whatever I forgot must be really important. I crank up the heater in my car and it becomes inhabitable after a few blocks. For a minute, I'm afraid that the whole thing feels a little planned-out. I feel like it's almost predatory for me to have arranged a date where we're outside and alone.

"I hope this is worth it," Tydomin says. "It's pretty

cold."

"I told you it was cold and I told you to get a hat."

She just rolls her eyes and sticks her fingers in front of the vents to warm them.

My old car couldn't have made it up the foothills nearly so well with the heater running. It was a pain in the ass to make that car try and perform two such tasks at the same time. This one doesn't have a problem and I honestly can't think if I've taken this car up into the mountains or anywhere near them since I got it. It's a relief that, when I feel like it's going to start letting me down, it just keeps on up the hill.

"You cool with this?" I ask.

"With what?"

"Us, going up the hill, all of that. I don't want this to be at all creepy. I mean, we could watch a movie or have coffee or something."

"Derek," she says, "It was my idea. I invited myself along."

She was right about that. I had talked to her about my star-watching. I took an astronomy class that changed the way I saw the night sky. I started thinking about how entire belief systems used to be built on the way the stars moved and I realized that I didn't the name of a single star. As I learned more, I started keeping track of celestial events like meteor showers, and now I didn't miss a single one of them as long as the night was going to be clear.

"I used to live up this way; right up this road for 40 miles or so" Tydomin says. "Way in the Sequoias."

"We won't go that far," I say.

"How many do you think we'll see?" She asks.

"You tell me."

"How many did you see last year?"

"I didn't go last year," I say. "I saw a good one in August and it was breathtaking."

There's a long road off of the main highway at about 3000 feet of elevation. It's far enough out of Ashlan that the city's lights don't bother you there. The night is clear, so it's extra cold, and the stars are spread out above us when I turn off the car and we step outside. The air is crisp and it's quiet. I pull a sleeping bag out of the trunk and spread it on the ground. I pull another sleeping bag out to put on top of us.

"Don't you go getting ideas," Tydomin says.

We climb into the sleeping bags and she slides next to me and gets settled with her head half way on my arm and half way on my chest. It's just then that I see the first shooting star run across the sky.

"Wow," Tydomin says. "It's beautiful."

We watch as the meteors, just specks of dust and

debris, run long streaks, one after the other, across the canopy of stars. I can feel the energy of the show reflected in Tydomin's body. She's thrilled and awed by the trails that they leave behind, pieces breaking off and falling in brilliant fires.

The Gemonids are maybe my favorite meteor shower to watch. They come around at a time of year when I feel like I'm not getting outside enough and when I need to be reminded that the outside world has beautiful things in it. I never have watched them with a girl cuddled into me before and I can't help but notice that I'm not watching the shower much, but watching the girl watching the shower.

"This is amazing, Derek," Tydomin says. "I mean really, really beautiful." She rolls over onto her elbow and pushes up so that she's looking down at me. I see her face, barely visible in silhouette against the stars spread out behind her. Her eyes glisten in the darkness and I see in them something I can't remember ever placing in a girl's eyes before; desire. I remember Vic explaining this look to me years before. "It's like a twinkle in their eye," he said. "It's like an inspired look of just plain wanting you. And they can't control the look. They can't make it if they don't want you, and they can't hide it if they do. And if you see it in a girl's eyes, you'll know exactly what to do about it."

I don't do anything but look at her. I try really hard to see this moment for all that it's worth and recognize that I'm enjoying it. Before I know it, she bends forward and I feel her fleshy lips against my own. She stays, lingers, and I think to myself that I never thought that kissing could be so engaging. *I'm not here*, I think to myself, *I'm just a physical expression of this kiss. I was brought into being when it started, and I will fade away when it ends. Don't let it end.*

But it does end, and I don't fade away. Instead I was given a pulse for what felt like the first time in my whole life.

"You're the most wonderful person I've ever met," she says to me. "You're gentle and caring and selfless."

I want to defend myself against this rather positive accusation. I want to tell her that it's not like I had this thing planned; it's not like I wanted her to see how well I could orchestrate something, make a night work so well to raise the passion of a woman. I just wanted to come out and watch the stars with her, to be with her and the stars and for us to be with each other. There was no motive, no agenda, just a desire to be with her.

Before I can say any of this, she is leaned forward again and we are kissing and through my still-opened eyes I see two shooting stars scrape the sky at once and I feel like this moment was the only reason I was ever born.

December 9, 2006

The car ride back from the foothills is quiet. Again, there are the sounds of recorder, harp, and dulcimer softly interpreting familiar Christmas songs. The defroster is on full-blast trying to ward off the encroaching fog on the window. But the streets are uncharacteristically void of fog. The orange street lights shine down clearly on the road in front of us. There are no other cars that we can see at this time of night, long into the next day.

I'm sleepy, and can't wait to crawl into my little bed and I'm oh so grateful that I won't be going to school in the morning. I'm hoping my parents are asleep enough to not hear what time I come home.

Suddenly, without noticing it, I'm crossing Chestnut on Palm. I'm driving the same path that the car that his us drove, and I don't think I've been anywhere near this intersection for a year. If there was ever a call to drive this way, I avoided it. I can understand why now, because all of a sudden I have this pang of sorrow.

"Holy God," Tydomin says. "Are you okay?"

And I notice for a moment that I'm not exactly okay. I feel really sad.

"Can you stop the car?" She asks.

"Why?"

"Stop."

I pull the car over right in front of the intersection.

"This is where it happened," she says quietly. "I can see you, collapsed in your seat, covered in glass. Your nose is bleeding and you can't quite see. You reach over to him and you think that maybe he's going to be okay. The other car shoots into reverse and then drives away fast. You shake your brother's shoulder, but he doesn't move. You start to cry."

And I notice that she has started to cry.

"Who told you?"

"No one," she looks at me with pain in her eyes. It's the opposite of what I saw in the darkness under the stars. She looks at me with pity and sorrow and it makes me feel like I've done something wrong. "I can just see it." She's crying now and telling me how sorry she is. How it wasn't my fault.

"It doesn't matter if it was my fault or not," I tell her. "It happened. It happened and I can't get away from it."

She shook her head. "No, you can't." She wraps

186

her arms around me and sobs into my shoulder. "I'm sorry, Derek, I'm so sorry."

It wells inside me, just how sad I am about Vic, and it bursts out. We are a stopped car with two people inside, deeply in love, crying.

March 16, 2005
Vic was a good sport to come along with me. I hate driving at night in this thick fog. For whatever reason, it feels a lot more bearable when you're at least not lonely in the car. Ashlan gets a layer of fog that really can't be believed by most people for much of the winter. There have been times when I have literally not been able to see my hand in front of my face. And to think that people go driving in it. It just doesn't make any sense at all.

I had to pick up an assignment from a guy in my biology class in the middle of this soup. We have been working on this group report for three weeks and it's finally time for me to pull my shit together and get my part of the work done. I don't like this Travis guy from class anyway, and when he called whining about how his Internet was down and I was going to have to come and get the disk from him, I wanted to beat the dude senseless.

I grab my keys and as I'm opening the car door, Vic

runs out and hustles over to the passenger side.

"I thought you had practice tonight," I say.

"I just called it off," he says. "I wanted to come along, get out of the house for a while."

I shrug and he gets in.

"You'll get the hang of this fog, bro," he says to me. "It took me forever. I mean, how long have you been driving."

"I don't know, six weeks?"

"See. You're doing fine for six weeks. Just fine."

The drive is quiet for a while. Unusually so. Vic never, ever, rides in a car without a CD playing. He's looking off in the distance to his side, even though there's nothing to see but fog.

"Anything going on, Vic?" I ask, more to break the silence.

He shakes his head. "I don't think so."

And it's quiet again, me concentrating on the road, shrouded in a cloth of fog, him looking out his window. I start to wonder why he came along in the first place.

"You know, bro," he says all of a sudden. "Things have been rough lately."

"How do you mean?"

"Not with you, nothing like that," he says. "I feel like I've been going down a bad road. I feel like I can't face Mom and Dad about a lot of it. I dropped all my classes this semester and haven't had the guts to tell them. In fact," his voice gets weak, "I spent the money I got back from the classes and shit I shouldn't be spending money on."

We let that hang in the air, the two of us, for several minutes.

"And?" I finally say.

"I feel like I want a do-over. A motherfucking do-over, you know?"

I glance at him, there's tears going down his face. I'm shocked; everything seemed fine, just a few minutes ago, he was fine. I've always envied him, wanted to be like him, wanted his life in so many ways. And here he is, out of the blue, telling me things have fallen apart in his world. I'm embarrassed about the whole thing and just wish he didn't come along for the drive.

"I think I made up my mind about things."

"In what way?" I ask.

"In every way," he says. Then he turns away from the window and smiles at me. "And I have to say that it just feels good to know what I'm doing with myself for once."

As he says this last line, I look over at him. We're crossing an intersection and out of the white darkness behind the passenger side window, a pair of headlights quickly materializes and then snaps into Vic's door.

When you're in a car accident, your senses shatter into pieces. All of a sudden you don't process the world around you as one cognitive structure, but as a collective of inputs all coming through on different wavelengths.

Sight is first for me. I see the headlights appear out of nothingness. I can see that they are higher off the ground than ours would be and farther apart, fitting almost he whole door of my Saturn between the two of them. Everything shakes at this point and after a blur of dense colors, I see my window get close and then break into a map of spider web cracks. The world out side the windows is spinning lights masked by the thick fog. The steering wheel comes up towards my face, splitting in the middle to reveal a white explosion of plastic cloth. The spinning comes to a stop. The bag deflates.

The sounds seem to happen all on top of each other. A boom, a bounce, a shatter, and the sliding sound of the tires against the street as the strain to resist being torn. This is all against the backdrop of screaming. The screaming, I can't tell if it's mine, my brother's, or both. Probably both.

Taste makes the quick transition from cinnamon gum to a chemical powder from the airbag to the metallic taste of blood.

The smells drift from the pine air freshener to a blast of nitrogen gas and sodium azide to the sweet smell of the leaking coolant surrounding the car.

Feeling is the worst. One moment I'm comfortable in my seat warmed by the heater. Then we are pushed to the left and our forward motion stops altogether. The seatbelt hammers against my body and the airbag hits my face at over 200 miles an hour breaking my nose. My arms and legs flail around me, my knee rips into the keys in the ignition opening a gaping hole in my pants and my skin. The cold air invades the cab of the car.

Within a second after the car stops moving, these five separate worlds of the senses come back together. I see the large white SUV that hit us drive off down the road quickly, hardly damaged at all. I look over at Derek, whose body is contorted in a disturbing pose and whose seat seems to have been pushed a foot closer to me.

"Jesus, Vic," I hear myself say. "Are you okay?"

"Fine," he says barely moving his lips. "I feel fine. Where are we?"

I put my hand on his head and try my hardest to keep my eyes open. I want to be with my brother for what are surely his last moments.

"Vic," again, it's more like I'm hearing this than saying it.

But he is already gone.

***

Sorry to butt-in again, but you should know this: how Vic had felt about himself was a secret he only kept with one other person, and he didn't even know that she knew. When Tydomin first saw Vic (in the flesh), she was shocked at how she felt about it. She didn't instantly regret what was going to happen to him; she had known that for a while now and expected it. She was shocked at how sad he had been in his life.

Tydomin had moved down to the valley and into an apartment with a girl she barely knew only hours before. And she knew that Erica was good friends with Vic. Erica thought the world of Vic, as a matter of fact, and much of her recent history was intertwined with his and with Abigail's, all at the same time.

But the picture she had of him in her mind, the picture of a passionate person and musician who lived a carefree and happy existence wasn't there; at least it wasn't according to how she saw him when she *felt* his past. Instead, he was a disappointed in himself. He was something he didn't want to be—unreliable, flippant, arrogant—and nursing a recently developed methamphetamine habit. The meth, she could plainly see, was something that no one of his friends knew about; something he harbored guilt upon guilt about.

193

And things weren't likely to get better, she could plainly see. Before he had a chance to clean-up, to make something of himself, he would be killed. And he would be killed because of something *she* had done. He would be killed because she had challenged who *she* was. It was something so twisted up inside of her, that she couldn't focus on it herself. It was something so wrong, it didn't agree with how she saw the world. She couldn't face it. She had to consider an alternative, somehow.

It was really wrapped up like this: she tried to change something, and if that *failed*, she would have known she never would have been able to save her parents. But its success showed a totally new reality, shed new light on who she was and what motivated her. Its success let her see just how ugly it is to try and fight who you are. Tydomin wanted to kill part of who she was but it would end up killing him. He had become her sacrificial lamb. He expressed part of her that had to die: a part that was self-loathing, disappointing, regretful.

She thought it about it a lot over the coming weeks. She stayed in his circle, long after she didn't need to anymore, staying close to him. She watched for an opportunity to get to him alone, to try and talk to him and not mistakenly throw others off of their projected path. And one night, she saw her best chance. His band had finished playing, Erica and Abigail had left, and Vic packed up his gear. When he stepped outside to have a smoke, Tydomin approached him. She would take another crack at it; she would try and undo what she had done, unforeseen consequences or not.

sol smith

sight

chapter 7

Tydomin White

December 10, 2004

I'm painting in my art room. I could hardly be further away from Red's office, but still I'm quiet. I don't know if I'm quiet because I don't want to be heard or because I want to try and hear what's going on. I know that Red is locked in his office with that same stranger, a man who he doesn't want me to meet. He's been meeting with him every couple months ever since I moved in here. I still have never seen him and he still has never seen me, so far as I know. I don't know exactly what it is they're working on because Red won't talk about it at all. I know he's not a nice man, that's probably the only thing I know about him.

My understanding is that he's afraid that he'll give off the wrong impression, like when mom would drink behind my dad's and my back so that we didn't see that she thought it was okay to be drinking in the middle of the afternoon. I always knew when she did it, at least after the fact, because she would always be so sad and I would look at her with my feeling look just to see what it was that she was so sad about. If drinking by herself in the middle of the afternoon made her sad, I just don't know why she would do it.

I'm painting a picture of mom now. I'm looking backwards at myself and trying to see an image of her that I can paint. I'm much better at painting already. Like much, much better. Sometime, way in the future, I take art classes. Red has helped me to see them already; to feel the skills I will learn in my fingers already. It took me a really long time to do, I kept getting caught up in how old I was and what I was wearing in each vision. It hurt my head a little to do and I had to take lots of breaks to do it.

Red said that it's the key to seeing. He said that no one at his old job ever knew just how far into the future he could see. He said that because he made it a part of his daily life to explore what he saw in the future, he opened windows into the past where he could look forward and see the visions of the present.

It makes my head hurt to think of. But this is the kind of thing that Red and I work on all the time. A vision of a vision of a vision. Most of it is things that are just too remote for me to see. And I don't work on it like Red does and I know I don't even work on it as much as Red wants me to. So there are missed opportunities every day that I don't spend a good amount of time looking forward to the future. I can never see it from the past if I don't look at it now.

My painting of mom is coming along very well. I've noticed that when I paint a picture of someone from my past, I use long and gliding brush strokes. I spread the color across the page and let it begin and end in ambiguous places. When I look at the completed picture, I'm never quite sure where one brush stroke ends and where the next one begins.

So far, the best picture I've painted, I painted yesterday. I spent all day long on it. It was one of the few times when I painted a picture of something that was just sitting right here in the present with me. I woke up, looked outside, and saw the trees covered in fresh snow. I set up a canvas in my room and looked out the window all day long making that world stay still and stay put on the canvas. I looked out over the hills all the way down into the valley and I tried to make those trees come to life and stay with me.

Somehow, though, the trees made me feel lonely when I looked at them. I never grew up around the snow and my parents only took me up to the mountains once to play in the snow. All of a sudden I realized where I was, sitting in a huge bedroom in a house that isn't really my own, looking out at this beautiful sight that's not really mine to see. My life, I finally thought, is borrowed. I'm just sitting here in the middle of it for one second, and I'm going to go off to other things the next, and when I look back, that one second won't even seem like it happened.

I've already seen that I'm going to be moving away soon. Less than a year. I'm not sure how much less, because every time I start to see it—which is more and more—I realize that I don't want to see it, not yet. I'll be living with someone, a girl, in a small apartment in Ashlan. Starting over again.

I wonder how many more times in life I have to start over.

Red said it was a huge step forward to paint a picture of something from my present. He's always told me that it's important for seers and feelers to locate themselves in their lives. The present is hard to find, hard to stay in.

While I've noticed this, I've noticed something else, too. I've noticed that no matter how many times I see the future and look out at a beautiful view—trees, sunsets, clouds, stars—I'm never ready for it when it comes along. All of a sudden I'm there and looking at this view and I feel my heart bounce around inside me. I'm inspired by the colors that a setting sun paints on the trees and rivers. I'm moved by the way a strong wind bends the world of branches over in a flowing dance step. It's exciting to me beyond words, and I think more exciting for me than for some people because I've spent so long looking at these things from afar, and all of a sudden the present is *there* and I'm there with it.

I look at my painting of Mom and it makes me sad. I put my brush down on the easel. I don't want to work on it any more, yet I feel this sense of duty.

Duty to the future. I can see that I spend the rest of the afternoon painting this picture.

This happens to me once in a while. I'm struck at first by how absurd it is that I'm going to sit here and do this just because I can see that I'm going to make the choice to do just that. Again I'm struck by the idea that I should walk downstairs, through the halls, across the living room, and march into Red's office. Then I'd meet this man he meets with and be done with the whole damn thing. I will have exerted my free will and I could go back to living life like normal. If I could just see how much of my life I can change. If I could just know if there was anything I could have done...

I push my chair back and look at the door. I'm going to do it.

I walk to the door and turn the knob. I look back at

the painting. I go down the hall and stand for a minute at the top of the stairs. It's quiet down below and I get an ominous feeling just looking down. I think, don't look forward, don't look forward. I'm scared to think of what I would see if I try looking into the future. My mouth is dry and I convince myself that I'm just headed to the kitchen to get a glass of water. Maybe I am, it's not like I have to go Red's office.

I walk down the stairs quickly. I'm in another hallway with tile floors and a door at the end of it going into the living room. I open the door and walk through the living room and glance over at the piano. Oh my God, I think to myself. I'm going to do it. I'm going to change the future.

This is something small, insignificant, really. Walking in on a meeting in Red's office, nothing in the scheme of things. Yet, is something Red knows I won't do, so if I can change it, I can not only change *my* visions, but Red's as well. Small, I know, and important.

I get to Red's office door. I stand for a long time, looking at the knob. My heart is in my breath. I dare to look forward, into the future.

I see myself sitting at the easel, still working on the painting of Mom.

This is a really bad idea. I shouldn't be here. This doesn't happen. I make up my mind to turn around.

Then.

The doorknob turns and the muffled voices from behind the door get louder. I'm frightened and I stand still, looking in disbelief at the opening door.

A tall man with very short black hair wearing a business suit looks at me with surprise. More surprised, Red stands behind him.

There's a sudden, splitting headache that blinds me. I scream. I collapse to the floor.

The man picks me up and brings me to my feet. "Are you okay?" Behind him, Red holds his head, buckled over. He stands up quickly. And I see his face strain with pain, though he never makes a sound.

I can't talk.

"Who is this, Red? Should we get her to a doctor?"

"Don't worry, Alan," Red says. "This is my niece. She's staying here temporarily. She hasn't been feeling well."

I nod my head vigorously.

"Why don't we lay her down on the couch and I will walk you to the door?"

The tall man picks me up in his arms and puts me on the couch. "I'm sorry if I scared you," he says to me. "I hope you're alright."

I can barely muscle out a "thank you" and Red leads him to the door.

Red Scabergrade

December 10, 2004

Alan and I are going over the latest set of blue prints
I've made for his project. Over the years, he has made
more money from my maps of the future than he
could have ever dreamed. And he has paid me more
money than I could spend in what's left of my lifetime.
The trick to getting money from big spenders like this
is to keep them constantly looking for the next score
instead of just looking at this one. I introduce another
set of perimeters with each meeting that will advance
his control based on what he has done already. In
actuality, most of the work after the first stages is work
he could have done himself as a business man. But he
feels that by prognostication, he is taking all the guess
work out. But his future would be his future if I was
seeing it or not.

"These look very good, Red."

"Of course. But you have to get on this right away.

We have a whole different round coming up in February," I tell him. "And what happens in this next election can greatly affect your bottom line. Interest rates, I'm sure you know, are going to be a huge concern of yours."

He nods and smiles. He starts to gather up the papers to put into his case. Then he pulls out his check book. "How much for this round?"

I sit back down in my chair. "Alan, how long have you been in the real estate and insurance business?"

"Long enough."

"You don't come about this by the natural means. You yourself told me that you used to work for the Agency. Might I inquire what branch or discipline?"

His eyes narrow. "Why do you ask?"

"I think that I know what line of business you've been in. And I don't know if you've given it up entirely yet."

"What line would that be?"

"Alan," I say calmly. "I think I know a way that you can cut your expenses on this project. In fact, you could cut your expenses on any *future* projects that you have with me."

He looks at me and sits down.

"I don't think that Ann was the one who pointed you in my direction."

"Red," he says. "We've been working together for years. You do trust me, don't you?"

"Of course."

"Ann sent me."

I shake my head. "No. You've heard some rumors. You have some information from someone inside the Agency. You've heard this idea that I was holding back, that I have information the Agency still wants. And I don't know if you plan to collect that information for them or there's a private contractor behind it all."

"I don't know what you're talking about."

"Andy Devidjian does. Little guy, about 50, runs the head shop in Merced. Ring a bell?"

"No."

"I've known about Andy for years. He used to work for the peripherals in the Agency as well. He did his job well. Especially his embassy work, but he spent a lot of time in the heads of the seers. He knew about the project that I worked on in my spare time at the Agency and he thinks he can get a good price for it.

"But this is something you should know about these telepaths. They cannot be trusted. They're full of tricks. Andy would just as soon kill you as pay you for what he's asking from you."

"And what," Alan says, "Do you think he's asking from me?"

"He wants you to get a hold of something from me." I stand up and walk to the closet. I open it, revealing a safe. I type in the code and swing open the heavy metal door. I pull out a stack of six CDs in cases. "This is a map of the next 200 years or so of human history. Major political movements, cultural movements, natural disasters, wars, you name it. It is done in great detail. It's categorized, mapped out, everything. There are schematic for patents that will be of great concern. This doesn't ring a bell?"

I see in Alan's eyes a light. This is exactly what he's been looking for this long while. I've kept him happy bringing him a hearty income with what he thought was his cover for this operation.

"Speak now, Alan."

"Yes," he says. "I do work with Mr. Devidjian. He hired me away from the Agency for this job." He is nearly whispering. "What are you doing, showing this to me?"

"How much did he offer you for this?"

"More than I've made with you."

"Do you know why he has offered you that much?"

"I imagine he plans to turn around and sell it."

"Do you know who he is going to turn around and sell it to?"

"The highest bidder?"

"That's right," I say. "When I worked for the peripheral department in the CIA, I did not give them everything that I could have. I gave them what was expected of me. But the truth is, as far as I can see, there's never been a seer quite as skilled as I am. They had no idea what I was capable of."

"That's the rumor."

"Do you know how that rumor got out? It was Andy. Devidjian worked as a telepath, doing his share for the CIA and the State Department. Our paths crossed once and he turned his abilities on me. He saw the wealth of knowledge I was able to gain using my talents and using the resources that the CIA offered me. I learned about his scheme because he has a big mouth. My friend who still works at the agency, Eric Night, told me all about it. Do you know Eric?"

Alan is still on the edge of his seat. I'm afraid he's looking for the opportunity to take this from me. But I can see that he won't. "I worked with him a little. Desk jockey, right?"

"Right. Eric has his sources. And he has warned me about you. And I just think that you should know that Devidjian isn't planning on keeping you around."

"Let's not get to melodramatic here, Red. He hasn't given me any reason not to trust him."

210

"Of course not, he's a telepath! Telepaths specialize in gaining trust. You have very little defense against him. And he will kill you the minute that you hand this over. I have never steered you wrong. And despite what Devidjian tells you, he is no psychic; he has no ability to see the future. Trust me, he plans to kill you."

"Who is he going to sell to?"

"You want me to give this to you and you'll just cut out the middle man? I will let you in on everything I know, Alan. But not with Devidjian in the picture. I know that he can't be trusted. You take care of Devidjian, and I'll hand this over. As long as he's around, there's no way. I hardly care about this stuff anymore, and I've become convinced that it's no good to anyone who does buy it; either the future doesn't change once they have it, and there's no threat, or it does change just by virtue of their possession, and there's no threat. But Devidjian, he has to go. "

"I owe him a lot," Alan says. "So I don't see how you're going to trust me. What can I do to show you that he's out of the picture?"

"That, Alan, is up to you. But until you've proven this to me, our relationship must be on hold."

Alan nods. I can see that the seed has been planted and that all of this unpleasantness will soon be behind us. Without saying a word, we both stand up and walk to the office door.

"I'll come back," Alan says as he opens the door. "Once I have this whole thing figured out."

Suddenly I feel as if I've been struck in the head by a sharp object. The door to the office swings open, and Tydomin, standing on the other side, screams and gasps her head. She falls to the ground, but I maintain my composure. I explain to Alan that she is only my niece who doesn't feel well and was supposed to be in bed; my sister is out of the country.

Alan picks the girl up and puts her on the couch, still clutching her head. He leaves without saying much about it, but I can tell that I have a lot of work to do to catch up with this change.

Tydomin is in pain, lying on the couch. I don't reproach her, she knows that she wasn't supposed to see him, and, more importantly, that he wasn't supposed to see her. "The headache is from changing the future," I tell Tydomin. "Neither of us will be able to process this change until the pain subsides to some degree."

"I am so sorry, Red."

"Don't worry about being sorry. We have to worry about whether or not this is going to put you in danger down the road."

"What kind of danger?"

"He may not have looked like it, Tydomin, but Alan is a very dangerous man. Just relax, I'll get you some water, we'll wait. We'll assess the situation before we get all panicked about it. I'm sure everyone is going to be just fine."

Martin Oaks

December 12, 2004

"This is a complicated situation, Mrs. English. It's a good thing you came to us."

"Of course," the woman says, "I usually only speak to Delphi, so I would like to hear his opinion on it."

"There's really no need, Mrs. English. Delphi is going to tell you the same thing that I do, but I'm going to be more honest. Plus, he's out of town. And, you save 10% by going through me instead of Delphi."

"Cost," Mrs. English says, "is not what is important here, young man. Are you cheaper because you're not as good?"

"Have a seat, Mrs. English," I say. "I will show you how good I am. And, under the circumstances, I feel that you are in dire need of someone to help you. This can't wait until next Thursday, when Delphi gets back."

Mrs. English is a rich woman. She was raised in a superstitious household, which helps, and married into

214

money, which also helps. She's been coming to Andy for years and he's trying to pawn her off on me. I don't like her, and in fact, she's one of my least favorite types of people. She doesn't trust her husband, who works a lot and pays a lot for her to have the lavish lifestyle that she lives. And despite that, she comes here week after week to find out what's happening with her husband; is he cheating on her, is he losing his job, is he impotent, that kind of shit.

Now, granted, a lot of this is Andy's fault; he makes a living by stealing irrational fears out of her head and feeding them back to her. Andy recruited me to do the same thing. It's good money and it's nice to spend time with someone else—however petty and reclusive—who can read minds like I can.

"I'm sensing something," I say with my blind eyes closed for effect. "I'm sensing a man in a brown suit, balding, working as an attorney."

"Yes," she says, "that's my husband. What is he doing?"

I act very surprised. "Your husband? Are you sure?"

"It sounds like him. What's his name?"

"Hold on, it's coming through," I squint my eyes now. "Hearing things can be hard. Hold on. Hold on. Norman. His name is Norman and he's wearing a white

215

gold ring on his left hand with two little diamonds set in it where three once sat."

"Oh my God," Mrs. English says. "That's him. That's Norman. You have to tell me Martin, what is he doing?"

I'm amazed at how pathetic this woman is. She's excited that I know something that Andy very well could have told me. A little pomp and I could convince her of anything. "I'm afraid you don't want to know," I say.

The woman's mind races. Everything she is afraid of hearing goes through her head as fast as she can think of it. Finally I settle on a thought.

"Please," she says.

"Okay," I act reluctant. "I'll tell you. He's cheating on you."

There is a gasp. "He *is*?"

"Yes."

"It's that secretary, isn't it? That damn slut."

"No."

"Who?"

I almost make myself laugh by thinking of saying, "your mother," but I get control of myself. "I'm afraid that's the part I don't want to tell you," I say.

"You have to, Martin. I'll pay you double. I have to know."

I rub my temples, mystically. "His name is Chase. He is also a lawyer."

"Chase? His partner?"

"Are they partners? I'm so sorry to tell you this, Mrs. English. And it looks like their whole firm is in on this. Shame."

"It just can't be true."

I look at her as solemnly as I can. Through her eyes I can see a look of earnest sincerity, like a priest giving the hard truth of gospel to a sinner. "Mrs. English. We can't understand the ways of the wicked. It may not seem to make sense to you, but that is because you are a good, reasonable person." I reach out and hold her hands in mine. "You've come to trust us here, and that we can help you is a good thing. If I were you, the first thing I'd do is go out and get myself tested. There's no telling how many horrible diseases he's brought into your house. Get tested and get him tested. Keep up to date about vaccines and STDs and stuff like that. Read some medical journals, that would be a good idea. Cover to cover."

"This is too much," the woman sobs. "I don't know what I've done to deserve this."

"For one," I say, "you don't trust him. You come here and have us keep on eye on him. You could be spending more time being a good wife, for example."

217

"You don't understand," she starts to say.

"I don't care to understand, Mrs. English. You go and see if you can get your life back together. Come back when you have your shit together."

She storms out, understandably so. As soon as the door to the shop closes, the door behind me opens. Out comes Andy Devidjian, breathing fire at me, as I thought he would.

"What is wrong with you, Oaks? How long have you been here?"

"Six months."

"And in six months you haven't gotten a clue about what we do here?"

"I know exactly what we do here," I tell him. "We take people's insecurities, exploit them, and make them give us their money for doing it."

Andy huffs at me, like I'm a child who just doesn't understand. "We get them to come back, you dumbfuck. That's the most important part, that they come back to spend money again. If we can't get them to come and spend their money again, we have no business. Martha English has been about the most consistent client we've had for the last few months and you go and feed her some total bullshit about her husband being gay? Are you taking this seriously at all?"

I laugh because it sounds so funny coming out of his mouth. "Oh come on, Andy. She's a total bitch who I can't stand being around. I'm glad she's not coming back."

"This is bullshit, Oaks. I should have left you in that asylum to rot."

I flip Andy off, which is pretty effective since the guy can see pretty well for someone who is severely telepathic. I pretty much think that you can measure a person's telepathic power by how well they can see. If they haven't come to totally rely on telepathy and forgotten how to see, they can't have too good an ability to begin with. At least in my mind.

He storms back into his office and I slunk onto the couch. Andy thinks I owe him so much because he helped me get out of the institution where my mom put me. I was never convinced that I should try and prove to anyone that I wasn't crazy. Andy comes along, senses someone like him, and gives in to his savior complex.

The truth of the matter is, I liked it in there. When Mom was through moving around, running away from the problems that I created for her, she put me there. She had heard it was good, she told me. She had heard that they could help me. They were a good Catholic hospital and she knew that I would find the help I needed there. She was tried to convince me that after a few months of treatment, I would be better. I might even have my sight back. That's what the doctors had told her.

But what I read in Mom's mind was totally different. She was going to be relieved. She was going to be thrilled to be rid of me. I heard the same laughter of relief ringing in her mind that she had when she ridded herself of Max. The same kind of relief was going to wash over her. And this time, she didn't have to push her child underwater and feel the convulsions of the child trying to survive.

There's a knock at the door, and as far as I can remember, there are no more appointments today. I look past the door for a mind to inhabit, and I feel his hand resting on the handle of a gun in his pocket. It's that Alan guy who stops by to talk to Andy every goddamn month or so. He is usually packing some kind of weapon, but I get the distinct impression that he's up to something this time and has in him some kind of intent to use it.

I answer the door. "How can I help you, Alan?"

"You can point me in the direction of Andy."

"Yeah, I can." I lift my arm and point in the direction of the office. "Alan," I say as he starts to walk past me. "He has got to know by now what's in your pocket. He's not a moron, you know."

Alan walks by anyway, and as he gets to the office door, three holes poke through from the other side. The sound of the gunfire is sudden; a popping that's loud and staccato. I fall to the ground and crawl behind the couch. From where I am, I flip back and forth between the minds of the two other men in the shop.

Alan is on the ground, too, absolutely quiet, out of the way of the door. He wasn't hit with the volley that Andy fired. He's calm, calculating his next move. He's going over the layout of the shop in his head, looking for other points of entry to Andy's office.

Andy, however, is reading his mind and deciding if he's going to rush through the door while Alan is planning. His original idea of catching Alan off guard didn't quite work out. Even with what sight he has, he just can't aim well enough for this fight, and he knows it.

Andy calls out, "What the hell, Alan?"

"We're through, Andy," Alan yells back. "I'm taking it for myself."

Of course I know exactly what it is that they're talking about. That damn map that that psychic guy has southeast of here. It's all they ever talk about when they're locked in that office together.

"You don't know where to take the damn thing,

Alan. Don't make this mistake."

I rush through Andy's head as fast as I can. I see his connections the guy who he plans to sell the map to. "Um, Alan, for what it's worth, I know where to sell it," I chime in. "Andy is holding a .357 magnum and he has no more rounds for it after he spends these next three. I don't know if he's told you or not, but he can't see very well. I suggest taking care of this as quickly as you can."

"Shut up, Martin," Andy yells back.

"He's hiding behind the desk on the wall on your right hand side," I say. "He's pretty much scared shitless."

Before I can catch up with exactly what's going on, there is a scrambling sound and another volley of shots fired, these from Alan's gun which has some kind of silencer on it. He thinks so quickly in this situation that I can hardly watch him; his moves are so practiced and precise that I can't follow the process he uses in thinking. It's mechanical. He's a professional, no doubt about it.

Just as the last shot is fired, I switch my point of view and have The Spirit breath Andy's smoke into my head. I see through Andy's dim vision as the tall man in a leather jacket stands over him. Andy can't quite grip the gun, and the world is losing light very quickly. A thousand thoughts race through his head, and like a flame on a candle being chocked out by too much wind, his mind flickers out of existence. I am left with a void in my head that was once inhabited by Andy Devidjian. I can't decide how this makes me feel right off the bat.

Alan's attention is turned instantly to me. His hackles are still up, and his firearm is still raised.

"Don't worry," I call out. "I'm unarmed and I have no interest in fighting with you."

He is standing above me now; I can see through his eyes that I look pretty pathetic gathered into a clump behind the couch, eyes squeezed shut. His black gun is pointing at me accusingly, the silencer adding length to the frightening piece. "Suppose you start talking," he says. He's going over in his mind everything he thinks he knows about me. He sees me as Andy's smart-ass assistant. He doesn't feel that I'm a physical threat, but he is worried about the idea of witnesses.

"Don't worry," I say. "I'm totally blind." I open my eyes wide and look in his direction. From his vantage point, I can see that my eyes are empty and almost colorless. I look blind to me, at least.

"Don't pull this shit with me," he says. "I know your kind. You know exactly who I am and what I look like."

"Did I earn no points with you by telling you where Andy was?"

The gun makes a clicking noise, and I desperately dig through his mind, trying to find something, anything to go on. I see someone in a house, a girl that for some reason has a lot of questions around in her head about. "Why does he have that girl there, anyway?" I blurt out.

He hesitates. "Who? What girl?"

"Why is he keeping her secret?"

"Are you talking about Red?"

I have him, thank God, I have him. The knot in my stomach loosens a little. "I can tell you whatever you need to know," I say. "I can tell you everything he knew about this project of yours. I know where to sell the map, who to call and how much the damn thing is worth to the guy."

"You know where to find it?"

I think about this. No, I don't know where to find it. Andy didn't know where to find it. He wasn't even sure if it existed. He was too scared to get close to the seer to find out. Suddenly, I find myself in a position to negotiate. If I did know where it was, I was as good as dead when I talked. But this way, I can still provide a service.

"I can find out where to find it. I can. I swear. I know exactly how. Just let me live."

Abigail Winters

December 22, 2006

I saw Derek earlier tonight. It was before his girlfriend got off work so he had time to sit and talk with me. We talked about my relationship, how it had gone bad, how I didn't think I was interested anymore. It kind of hurt me that Derek sat there and listened to me and said things like, "Damn, I'm sorry," but never really offered me much in the way of a listening ear.

Derek can be like that. It's the age, I guess. Self-centered. He's a sweet kid, but as long as he's happy, as long as he's thrilled to be with this strange little girl, he can't seem to see the harm in the rest of the world. He can't put things aside long enough to just listen to me. He left when Tydomin got off work, but I'm still sitting here at the Andante, nursing a cup of hot tea.

It's not his job, I guess. It just has been for so long, I've forgotten how to live without it.

This morning I cut myself for the first time in a

long time. After Vic's death, I did it quite a bit. But with Derek and the support that he gave me, I noticed that I didn't need it so much.

I was lying on my bed, the morning light just coming through my dark blinds. I didn't want to wake up. I put my fingers on my chest and felt the old scars. This one, I thought, was Vic's death. It was long, it was deep, and it was my first one. Many of the ones I've done since then have healed and can barely even been seen, but that one can still be felt with the fingers.

I moved my hand to the left. I found another large one, the one I made when Erica left. Above that was my dad's wedding. Moving all the way across my chest, just under my right arm, was another deep one. It was when I moved out. I stood in my apartment, listening to the silence, looking at the stove that was heating a kettle for tea. The stove was old and electric. The coils, turned on high, were glowing red.

Running through my mind, over and over on a loop, I thought of taking that kettle off. I wanted to press my cheek against it. I wanted to feel it burn through my cheek and to hear the sound. I wanted to smell it. I wanted to by lying in bed with the burn swelling and pulsing on my cheek.

I wouldn't be lonely. Or at least I wouldn't *feel* lonely.

Then I thought of next time I saw Dad, I'd tell him about an accident that I had, that's why the scar. Every time I looked in the mirror, I would be reminded. All the pain would be moved from the inside to the outside. And it sounded like such a relief.

I took the kettle and moved it aside. I started lowering my face down to the burner. Then I burst into tears. I ran into my small bedroom and pulled the box of razors out from my closet. I took one and shoved it deep, until I felt my rib at the end. I dragged it, and felt the ripping, felt the tears running down my cheeks.

I thought of all this, lying on my bed this morning, and I dug through my closet looking for the shoebox. It was there, and inside were razors. I just wanted to have a little one, I told myself. A little one for a boyfriend who doesn't respect me, one for a friend too busy to hear about it.

I pressed the blade into my arm and felt the surface tension on my skin break. I laughed and pulled it back. Then I started to cry.

"Can I sit with you?" a voice breaks my concentration.

I look up and see that it's Dave. "Oh my god, Dave, sit down." I take my bag off of the other chair at my table. Dave puts his coffee mug down. "Who are you here with?" I ask.

"Oh, the band. They can talk without me for a while. That'll give them a chance to kick me out if they want."

"No one kicks a drummer out of their band in Ashlan, Dave," I say. "There aren't enough decent ones to go around."

Dave smiles. He's wearing one of those knit caps to keep his head warm in the cold. "How have you been, Abbie?"

"You know. Good."

"Really?" He pulls a cigarette out of his shirt pocket and lights it. "You sure?"

"Well," I say. "Things could be a little better."

"Yeah. I'm just guessing that you're not dating Brian anymore, right?"

I sigh. "I have no idea. We haven't really had a state of the relationship address any time recently. I'm thinking he'll show up here sooner or later. I think he works here tonight."

"Nah," he says. "I saw him over at Stone's. I don't think he's going anywhere from there any time soon."

"Really?"

"He hasn't been any trouble, right?"

I shake my head. "I really don't want you to get the wrong idea. He's a really sweet guy. I mean, I know he's a blow-hard and a hothead, but he's really sweet, too."

"He's not really sweet," Dave says. "I don't want to badmouth your boyfriend or whatever, and I don't mean to be an ass, but he's not sweet. He's a bona fide jackass."

I can't really tell why Dave would come over and be so brazen. The guys in Vic's band did used to treat me like I was some kind of kid-sister, even though I was their age. It's nice of him to act all protective, but he should also know when to just shut the fuck up.

"Maybe I'll go talk to him right now."

"Why?" Dave asks.

"See where things stand. Let him off the hook, if he wants off. See if things can be fixed of if I even want that. Christmas is coming up," I say. "I know it sounds stupid, but I don't want to be alone. My dad and step mom ran off to Mexico again for the holidays. So I'm left here, by myself."

Dave smiles. "Sorry I can't help you with that. But I can tell you it'd be better to be alone for it than to be with him."

"Thanks for the advice, but I think I can handle it." I give Dave a big hug and then take a big gulp to finish off the rest of my tea.

Walking down Olive, I look into the windows of all the stores along the street. An antique store, a board game store, the bookshop where Tydomin works. They're all decorated for Christmas, they all have strings of lights going from store front to store front. I can't help but imagine that in just a few days there will be people out here taking the lights down, dismantling the whole goodwill towards men thing. We'll be on another year and it will suck.

Walking into Stone's, I look up at the psychic shop upstairs. Maybe, I think, I should run this by Delphi before going in to see Brian.

Stone's isn't too busy tonight. I kind of hate hanging out at my place of work while I'm not working, because invariably someone from the staff will come over and start asking me questions about this and that and everything else. I don't mind answering them as long as I'm getting minimum wage for it. But as things stand, I don't get shit.

Sitting at his normal table in the corner, all by himself and a bottle of Corona, is Brian. I go over and sit down. "Hey," I say.

"There you are," he says. He's been drinking and I can tell. "I've been looking all over for you."

"Like all over the table, or what?"

"What?"

"Nothing," I say. "I was hanging out where you work. I thought maybe you'd come by." He's looking down at the table, like he's feeling bad about something. This must be one of those times where he drinks and gets all sad. I hate those times almost as much as the times when he drinks and gets all pissy.

"What's wrong?" I ask.

"Are you seeing that David guy?"

I slap my forehead in frustration. "Jesus Christ on his throne, no. How many times do I have to tell you that I'm not seeing him?"

"It's just that I haven't seen you in a while and I've wondered where you've been."

"You know where to find me four or five nights a week, right here. I think it's funny that you show up the one night that you *know* I have the night off. What's going on with you? That's a better question, don't you think?"

He looks up at me, then raises his Corona to take a couple fast gulps. "Can we go back to your place and talk about it?"

"I told you, Brian. I'm not really comfortable with being at my place right now."

"Come on. We need to talk somewhere private. We can get everything all out in the open without having all your coworkers sitting around watching us."

He's right about that last part anyway. "Okay, whatever, fuck it. Come on and I'll take you to my place."

"Will you drive?"

"I walked. Do you think you can handle walking a mile and a half?"

"Jesus. What-the-fuck-ever."

Derek Neely

December 22, 2007

"I just don't think it's going to work out, you know?" Abigail has been bitching about this boyfriend of her since I sat down, and honestly, it's just so damn boring. I just don't know why she has to torture herself over a relationship that sucks. Why can't she just drop it? Is she masochistic or something?

"I'm sorry to hear that," I say. "I really wish that it would work out for you, Abbie." I try and say this in a way that doesn't come across as high and mighty like I'm so great because I'm in a happy relationship.

"I mean, what do you think? Do you think I should *try*?"

Honestly, I've forgotten what the original question was, and I just don't get the impression that Abbie is looking for an honest answer. "Abbie," I say. "Just wish things were better for you. I don't know the guy, so I don't know. Maybe we can hang out tomorrow night and talk about it some?"

"What, when you're girlfriend is working late?"

"Yeah," I say. "I'm sorry, we have plans." I look at my watch and realize that it must have been a pretty insensitive thing to do.

"Fine, go on. Do whatever. You know where to find me tomorrow night. Sitting around waiting for you to come and bless me with your wisdom. Go ahead."

I try not to roll my eyes at her biting sarcasm. "Please don't be that way. I do want to talk to you, I really *do*. It's just that I really do have to go."

I feel like shit walking away, looking over my shoulder at her, head drooped, sitting by herself. As she always does when she sits at a table by herself, I see her take her purse-thing and put it on the chair I was sitting in. I think she hates to look like she's desperate for company or something.

I tiptoe upstairs to Tydomin's apartment. She lives in an old house that has been turned into several apartments. The bottom-floor apartment is where the landlady lives, and she's about 100 years old, literally. Tydomin told me to watch out for the old lady when I come and pick her up because she wouldn't approve of seeing me there. She only rents the other four apartments out to girls.

I knock quietly on her door and Tydomin opens it. "Hey," she says, "did you see Agnes?"

"No, I think we're in the clear."

"Yeah," Tydomin says. "I can hear her downstairs watching *Jeopardy*. She turns the TV up so loud that I've been involuntarily playing along."

I laugh at this and she shushes me.

"I'm just finishing something up, you want to come in to wait?"

"Yeah."

I've never seen the inside of Tydomin's apartment before. I always pick her up or drop her off and she keeps the door close to being shut behind her the whole time. Now inside, I can see what a beautiful painter she is.

The entire room is lined with her paintings. Many are hanging on the walls, but others are piled on the floor. In the far corner of the apartment is a twin sized bed. There's a desk next to it with a stereo on it, playing some modern classical music. She has two easels in the middle of the room, both with projects on them. Next to them is a large and tall table covered in pieces of wood.

"You can just sit on the bed," she says to me. "I just have a couple more joints to finish this frame. I have to have this one finished and up in the store this week."

She stands over the tall table with a desk lamp bent over her workspace. She is gluing little circles of wood into divots the very same size and shape in between two planks of wood.

"You make your own frames?"

"Mostly I don't frame them," she says. "But I try and frame up a few at a time. And making the frame is really the only way to do it." She very carefully wipes glue away from her little circle of wood.

"Which painting is it for?"

"That one; the one on the easel."

It's a painting of a face. The paint, for the most part, is all the same color a black with a few grey highlights. It's in the brush strokes, like rivers with strong currents moving within them. The currents come together, flow apart, and taken at once make a wonderfully expressive face.

"The light is just right on it right now," she says. "I have a spot in the bookstore where the light is just like that, so you'll be able to really make out the painting."

"I'm spellbound, Tydomin," I say. I tear my eyes away from that painting and look at the others around the room. They are all in different styles, different media, I suppose. Some of them are hard and angular, paintings of people and places that look absolutely

objective, real, with no softness to them at all. Then
there are others, like the one on the easel, that is all
shape and flow, with colors that are counter-intuitive
but lines and shapes that could have been painted by
clouds or blades of grass being blown by the wind.
"You are wonderful."

She looks at me and smiles. "Thanks, Derek." Then
she goes back to her frame. "There," she says after a
minute. It was a long minute where I found myself lost
again, prisoner to her painting on the easel.

She comes up behind me and wraps her arms
around me. I turn to face her and for a moment the
planets align for one of her kisses, pressed soft against
my lips. She holds my face and runs her fingers through
my hair.

"So," she says, standing very close to me. "What
are we doing tonight?"

"I was thinking that we would go to a movie," I
say. "But now I want to stand around and look at your
paintings for a while. How many do you have?"

"In this room right now?"

"Yeah."

"I'm not sure. About 45 or so?"

I look around the room again, I can see that in
some places on the floor, they are leaned up against
the wall four at a time. "That's quite an output," I say.

"How long have you worked on them?"

"Oh, I don't know. The oldest in here is probably 10 years old. But I don't keep all the ones I make. Some of them are just for practice, or I find them uninteresting when they're finished, or I keep them around for a while, then they seem irrelevant to me."

I walk around the room and flip through the canvases. I'm astonished at the care and skill that went into them. "Do you sell any of them?"

She laughs. "You can have pretty much any one of them you want, Derek."

"No, I mean, do you sell them like at craft fairs or online or anything? You could set up one of those Etsy shops online; people sell the most ridiculous things there."

"I'm not worried about them selling."

"So you're just going to keep painting until you have a collection of like a billion. I'm shocked at how much money must have gone into the production of all of these. You must expect some kind of return."

Tydomin sits down on her bed, which is neatly made, covered in an old quilt. Sitting toward the top of the bed, next to the pillow, is a raggedy old stuffed bunny. She picks it up and puts it in her lap. "I do expect a return, Derek, I just don't want to under price myself."

"So you have some confidence in your art?"

"Oh yes. And I know that it will sell and sell well. I'm just waiting for the right time." She walks around the room lighting candles and turning off lights. The room glows and shadows are painted on the walls, moving in the tide of candlelight. She wanders back around the room and sits down next to me again on the bed.

"There's a lot of people always waiting for the right time for something who never get anything done. You're still really young, Ty, and you should see that your age will serve you well in selling these things. You know, like some kind of human interest story where a young girl sells paintings that are so far beyond her age."

"I know," she says. She clutches the bunny that sits limply in her lap.

"So when is the right time?"

She looks at me as if this is a huge question I've posed. As if this takes some kind of answering beyond her measure of confidence. "Do you remember," she starts softly, "the other night."

I think back to the shooting stars, the kissing, the rediscovering of myself. But somehow, I feel like she's not planning on talking about that right now. I feel like she's probably talking about what happened next. I've been trying not to think about it, filing it away into my memory to try and make more sense out of it when things won't feel so painful for me.

"At the intersection," she says.

"Yes, Tydomin, I remember the other night," I sit down next to her. "I think about talking to you about it every day."

"There are some things that you should know about me, Derek. Some things that are going to be really, really hard to take."

She takes a deep breath. "Time is for me, nonlinear." She stops and looks at me, judges the expression on my face, which I leave as blank as I can. "It is laid out for me like a landscape. I can see ahead, at times several years ahead, and for some things only a few moments. But the events are stolid, stagnant and their relevance is sometimes unpredictable."

I nod, waiting to see where she's going.

"What makes the future real is a wave of emotion. Emotions ripens time, brings it to bearing the fruit of the present, where we tend to locate ourselves as creatures. We are emotional beings, people, so it is natural for us to feel most related to the spot of time where the emotion is at its ripest; where we can see and feel and touch it the most.

"I'm aware of the past, too. The very distant pasts

241

of people and places that I come in contact with. The emotion of the present has already been there, already ripened, and it is far past ripe in most instances. The past becomes sour, rotten, and most of the time sad for people. Even happy things are remembered bitterly through nostalgia. The happiness is empty now because the touchable emotion has moved on and all that is felt is the absence.

"What's worse is the bad things. Regret. Negative emotions rot much more quickly, and can burn a hole in the lives of the people who were connected with them. And once something gets far enough away, only the decay of the moment remains, and again we see the moment as irrelevant, as something that may as well not have happened and we detach ourselves from the distant past much as we do from the future."

She stops, looks at me wide-eyed. "Do you have any clue what I'm talking about?"

"That's kind of a steep question, Ty," I say. The light plays on her face, adding moving shadows. Somehow, the dim lights, the time of year, and the tone of her voice, somehow makes me want to believe her.

"Do you believe what I'm saying?"

There's a sincerity in her voice that I just can't let go of. Either she is truly out of her mind, or she really is some kind of psychic. Whatever the case, I can't forget the other night, the way I felt a wave of empathy from her, the way she seemed to feel exactly what I was going through as we came to that intersection. It was something that I hadn't talked about with anyone, really. I mean, she easily could have known where it all happened, but it would be much harder for her to guess exactly what it was that I was feeling.

"This painting," she says and stands up. She walks over to the face hidden deep within the strokes and currents of the paint. "Is going to change a lot for me."

"How so?" I ask.

"On Christmas Eve, a woman is going to buy this painting from me. She is going to pay what I frankly consider to be a ridiculous price. I've been looking forward to this for a long time, now. And I'm assuming that this event makes me happy, you understand, and that it is something that I want. I have always wanted my paintings to sell and I can see no reason why this sale would be a bad thing for me. But, again, I just can't see all the circumstances. I'm not as good as my mentor was. I can only see the big things, which, honestly, only constitute the 'small picture,' as it were."

"So a woman buys this painting from you? That's great."

"That's not all," she says. "She works at the San Francisco Museum of Modern Art. She ends up buying a second and third painting from me before she goes back up to the Bay Area. We make a deal and she puts these on display in a new installation.

"Again, there is no way I can reliably access the emotions that I will be feeling when all of this happens. But I can only assume that I will be ecstatic about the whole thing. It's a big deal to have paintings hanging there. At my age, considering I've had no showings and no reviews, it's huge. I mean, yeah, it's probably a lot of PR stuff, trying to discover someone who is a news story by themselves, a little orphan girl who paints good looking paintings and all of that. But regardless of the circumstances, it's really great. I mean, really great."

She says all of this like she's trying to convince herself of it. She's not overwhelmed or happy or excited. And she's a girl who gets really overwhelmed and excited about the littlest things. "Why aren't you more excited about this, then?"

She sits back down next to me and clutches my arm. "Two reasons. One, I'm never excited or dreadful about the things that I see coming to pass. I might get excited when they happen, but I find it absolutely impossible to be excited before the emotion hits."

"Okay, and two?"

"Because it's going to take me away from you."
The words she says hang in the air like icicles.

"Why is that?"

"You have to understand how big this is for an artist of my age. I move on. I move away. I'll have a fortune, practically, and be able to sell all over the place. I move up to San Fran, then the next year to New York. It's the easiest way to keep my career going. And to even have a career at this age is monumental. I get to do what I love—to paint—for the rest of my life. You know how big that is?"

"But what about *us*? I mean, isn't there something we can do?"

"I don't know, Derek. I don't *want* this to end. I don't ask for it. And I can't possibly tell you exactly why; if it's the distance or the lifestyle or what, I just don't know. Maybe we get in a fight, I can't tell. But I never wanted it to be this way."

"Tydomin," I say, my voice a little louder than it should be. "It's not fair of you to say these things. We don't have to break up. We don't have to do anything we don't want to, I don't care what you think is going to happen."

"I never meant to lead you on," Tydomin says. "You have to understand that I never meant to hurt you with any of this. It isn't my *choice* that things work out this way. It isn't something I can go around changing. You have to understand what the world is like for me, Derek. I couldn't have known that we would be in love."

I look at the painting, the face in the paint, and I feel distant and empty. I'm sitting in her apartment but I'm all alone. I've just been told by the only girl I can ever say I've ever loved that we have to go our separate ways because that's how she sees things happening. "Ty," I say. "It's not that I'm not excited for you or anything."

"Derek, I'm so sorry."

"I just don't know how to take this. You get me? I don't know how to take *any* of this."

"Don't think I'm crazy, Derek," her voice is starting to break and I'm afraid she's going to cry. "I can *prove* it to you. I can show you what I mean."

I shake my head. "No, I don't need you to prove anything. It's obvious to me that you at least believe this."

"It's true, Derek, I swear it."

"That's fine, I'm not worried about that. I'm worried about us."

She sinks down and grabs her stuffed rabbit and pulls it tight against her. "I knew I shouldn't have told you."

"It's not that, Tydomin. It's that you don't believe that our relationship is going to work. It's that you're not invested in it. You've been sitting around this whole time, feeling like I'm just someone to pass the time with. I'm someone who's not deserving of all your attention. You went into this knowing, I mean really knowing, that you were going to leave. I'm shocked."

"It really isn't like that," and now she's crying. And I don't feel nearly as bad about it as I thought I would. "You really need to understand."

"No, Ty, *you* need to understand. I might not be any kind of popular guy or talented, or anything else, but I'm deserving of your respect. The fact that I'm in love with you should show you that. You can change your mind about this. You don't have to be resigned to some kind of fatalism."

She buries her head into my shoulder, sobbing. "You don't think I know that? You don't think this is tearing me to pieces?"

I put my arm around her. "It's okay, Ty. You can change your mind. You can sell the painting, you can sell whatever and be in whatever show you want. Just don't move away until I'm ready to come with you. I can change my plans, go to college wherever you need to be. I mean, maybe we'll last that long, maybe not, but I think it deserves a chance."

"It does deserve a chance, Derek. But it doesn't get one. You go to college in Flagstaff; I'm off to other places."

"No. That's bullshit. You can change your mind and so can I. We can try. We don't have to discount this whole thing right now. We don't."

"I'm not discounting anything, Derek. I don't want you angry at me. But it's not like I can sit here and second guess my choices in life right now. I can't risk altering everything."

"Why not? It's something I have to risk every single day, isn't it?"

"It's different. It's different for you and me. I've tried before, the dumbest little change my mind could think of, and it ruined everything."

"So it can be done?"

"That's not the point," she says. "Changing things like that, it's not right. It's not natural."

"No, it's not natural to sit here and tell me these things. It's not natural for you to adhere to an arbitrary future that you think you see."

"I do see it, Derek. Trust me, I see it and I've seen it every day my whole life and it has dictated my life. It has torn my life apart. It has left me alone in the world."

"It has brought you to me, and that can make you be not alone. Can't it?"

"Derek, I'm not going to lie to you," her voice is barely audible. "I'm not going to change my decisions. And yes, my decision did lead me to you, very literally. I know I wouldn't be here unless I tried to change things that one day. That one little stupid change. But," and now she looks away from me. "It changed so much more."

"Like what?"

She turns to face me. "It killed two people, for one, Derek. Two people died to bring us together and I'm not going to risk it again."

"Is that," I ask, "how your dad died?"

"Yes, Derek. It's exactly how Red died, because of me. And the other person," she looks at me and stops talking. She just looks and I explore her face, the lines stretching across it, frozen in sadness, unable to speak.

"Who cares about the other person?" I say at last.

"Derek, I have to tell you."

"No, you don't. You don't have to tell me anything, I just want to know that you'll change your mind, you'll give us a chance. I'm not asking you to put aside your life or your ambitions or anything. I'm asking you to just not write us off."

"It's not a matter of putting those things aside.

There's more that you need to hear about this, Derek, sit down."

I notice for the first time that I'm standing up. "I don't want to hear any more about this right now. I need some time, I need to think, and I wish you would, too. If I mean anything to you at all, you'll think about what you're saying."

"You need to sit down, Derek, you need to hear what I have to say."

But it's too late, the door is closed behind me.

chapter 8

sol smith

Tydomin White

December 12, 2004

I'm painting in my art room. My headache cleared up late last night and I finally got some sleep. I haven't talked to Red since yesterday. He's been working in his office since it started. He said that his headache was splitting as well, but he didn't show it. And just as he said, Advil didn't do a thing to help. It just hurt and throbbed like I had an open wound for over a day.

"It's normal for us, our world has changed," Red told me. "Since half of what we are capable of perceiving is suddenly being reorganized, so are our synapses. It's a good idea for me to get to work now and explore the new landscape. There is no telling how far this change goes."

"Are you serious? One little thing? He saw me, big deal, right?"

"I'm afraid not, Tydomin. But don't be hard on yourself; this was my fault. I didn't explain the consequences of changing a decision. Never, not in all our years have I explained it. And I didn't tell you just how dangerous a man Alan is. But we have to deal with it. I'll look. You try and do something for your head. Maybe paint, maybe look back and feel some things. Just don't try looking forward, not yet. I'll tell you when I have everything figured out. I can deal with the pain, you can't. When the pain clears, you can start looking forward again."

The phone in Red's office rang after that. Red and looked at me and we both were surprised. This was it. The first thing in a brand new world for us. The phone rang. Neither of us had any idea it was going to happen or who it was going to be. He was calm, put his hand on my shoulder, then marched off to answer the phone. That was the last I've seen of him.

There's a knock on my door, though it is open. Red is standing there, looking concerned. "How are you?" He says.

"Fine. I feel better. I actually got a little sleep last night."

"That's when it cleared for me, as well. A day and a half of headaches. That's a big shift. Not the biggest I've ever seen, but it's big. And I'm afraid that it is a heavy shift for the two of us."

"What do you mean, Red?"

Red sighs and sits down on the chair by the door. "I'm afraid that two major things have changed in my life, Tydomin. One, I'm going to see my father tomorrow. And two, I'm going to be dying a lot sooner than I had thought."

I feel like the blood has rushed out of my head. "What?"

"I can't explain it all to you now. But we have to get you out of here before Alan comes back. And I have to convince him that you die along with me. It's the only way to keep you safe."

I can feel my eyes filling with tears. "Why, Red?"

"He has seen you. He is suspicious. He did what I had originally planned and he took care of a big problem for us yesterday. A problem that I'd rather you didn't worry about. But because he saw you, things went very differently yesterday. One change runs into another, and he approached something with a more open mind than he would have otherwise."

"We can both go, Red. We can both get out of here."

Red shakes his head and frowns. "We should have learned our lesson, Tydomin. We won't be changing anything else. This way, the way I have seen and mapped out, you will be safe. There will be some sacrifices, but you will be safe, and that's what's important. It's time that you looked forward. You will see what I have seen. The events of the future dictate our present, Tydomin. This is a change of plans, but it doesn't change what you can accomplish with your life. And that's really what this is all about."

"I don't want to hear this, Red. I'm numb, empty, heartbroken. You can't imagine how terribly I feel about this. You can't imagine how much my whole body aches to hear you say these things."

"Cheer up, Tydomin," Red says. "Remember, my death wasn't the only thing that changed. There will be good to come out of this for me."

Red Scabergrade

December 13, 2004

We drive down the mountains early in the morning. We take a different leg in the road than usual, turning north in Prather to go to Merced. Tydomin is quiet the whole way, hardly saying a word. It reminds me of the first car ride we ever took together, going the opposite way headed into the mountains.

We make it to Merced, and pick up this young kid, a psychic who was working with the now late Andy Devidjian. He called me a couple days ago; he surprised me with his call. The first way I had seen things pan out when Alan got to Devidjian's psychic shop, Alan shot both the psychics dead. I saw Martin's death as acceptable collateral damage. It got rid of all witnesses and took care of the last people who knew much about the map. Then, I was able to talk Alan into a full refund of all the services I've given him as thanks for a job well done.

But that doesn't happen now. Now things are

different.

Martin gets in the truck and Tydomin scoots over closer to me. I've never been comfortable with a telepath around. They're not to be trusted. That is the only thing I learned about them from working with them for years at the CIA. They only say things to serve their own interest, and they are always looking for ways to bed things in their favor. Martin is young, though, and inexperienced. Much like seers, telepaths need a good mentor to find their way through life and really learn their art. Martin's is dead. Though, something about him tells me he was much better than Devidjian ever was.

"Thanks for coming on such late notice, Mr. Scabergrade."

"Thank you for your call."

"Can I ask you, Mr. Scabergrade, what is this girl doing here?" I look over at the boy, sitting with his elbow hanging out the window looking straight ahead. "It's just that you never mentioned her on the phone. I don't know how I feel about someone else coming with us."

"She's with me, Oaks. She has her place in our activity today. Please, tell me which way to go."

Martin is paranoid. He is obviously trying to read me the entire time he's in the car. He's looking for the map, no doubt to tell to Alan. He could easily play this off as a nice and copasetic thing to be doing. But he know that I can see what is going to come of all of this, I suppose, so he's not pushing his luck by being overly polite. If there's one thing that telepaths learned about seers at the CIA, it was to stay away from them. Martin is either inexperienced or just backed into a hard place by being around me.

"We're here," he says. "I'm decently nervous about coming back here, Red. Can you tell me that we're going to be okay, that I'm not going to be held for any reason?"

I laugh at this a little and I look forward to when the three of us leave the mental hospital. I dwell on it for a moment, knowing that Martin must be scanning my mind.

"I see," he says at last. "Thank you."

We walk in and Martin explains who we are and says to the nurse that we'd like to see a resident by the name of Thrushgrove. The smile on the nurse's face drops when she hears the name and in its place is a sad little frown showing sympathy. "He's not doing well, I'm afraid," she says. "But I'm happy to show you to him."

We walk through some kind of a common room filled with crazy people. Their imbalance shows in everything they do, the way they walk. They are wandering around, working on different board games and different coloring books. "You've caught us at a good time," the nurse says over her shoulder. "This is the best time for visitors because the room is so full of activity. It's their free time. Buy Danny is over here."

We walk down a long white hallway lit with bright florescent lights. We walk into another room that looks much more like a hospital room. On a bed in the center of the room is an old man lying with his mouth wide agape. The nurse leaves us alone for a few minutes.

It is, without a single doubt in my mind, my father. I haven't seen him since I was young. But despite looking old and near death, he looks just like he used to. A whole world, a whole lifetime comes crashing back to me when I see him. I take a deep breath and remind myself that this is not the time to be angry. This is not the time to seek some kind of answer or lay some kind of blame. It's a time for me to say goodbye.

"Tell me, Martin," I say. "Does he know we're here?"

"He knows someone's here, Red."

"Can he understand what we are saying?"

Martin is quiet, his eyes are closed tightly. "It's hard to say, Red. He always used to understand what I told him, but now the stroke seems to have taken a lot of his most basic senses with him. Step closer to him, Red, let him see your face. Now step a little to the left, his right eye seems to be working much better than his left."

I do just as he says.

"There," Martin says. "He gets it now."

I look into my father's eyes, and they blink. I think I see him smile just a little.

"Tydomin," I say. "Tell me about him. Look back and feel."

The girl looks at him closely, like she's studying for a test. "He's been in here a long time, Red. Like 20 years or so."

"What about before then?" I try not to ask the questions I really feel like asking. I hope that Martin is deeply in Tydomin's head so that I don't have to censor my thoughts from him.

"He was sick, Red. He was very sick and out of money. He put you in the orphanage and never did anything but regret it."

I nod. It was more or less what I wanted answered.

"If it matters to you," Martin says. "He thought about it a lot when I knew him before." I can tell that Martin is extremely uncomfortable.

I walk to my father's side and press the nurse button by his bed. A woman comes and smiles at me with a sympathetic smile. "Nurse," I say. "I have a rather large favor to ask of you."

A few moments later, after letting Martin negotiate with the floor manager, a nurse and I wheel the piano from the common room to the side of the bed where my did is now sitting up. I take a seat next to him and I place his fingers against the keys.

"Only the one hand is going to work, sir, if at all," the nurse reminds me. It is very well, as I will be his left hand. I start to play, slowly, a tune that he used to play when I was younger. It's a ragtime tune by Joplin, one of his slower ones. After a few bars, his fingers press against the keys clumsily and he picks up the tune as well. We play the song through, then we play it again. I start to try and play a different one, but he plays the first again, and I join him.

We play through six more times, the broken and disjointed Joplin tune. For a few moments, the world slips away from me and I am firmly grounded in the present world. Our two hands work together to push into life a single tune. The only way that the two of us ever did communicate when I was younger was through the playing of a piano. And now I feel young again, and much like things were back then, I don't want to stop playing; I don't want to try and relate to him on any other level.

At ast we leave the institution and the car ride to Martin's apartment is absolutely silent. When we get there, I tell Tydomin to stay in the car, that I have business with the boy.

"How much do you need?" I ask him.

"I need a good start, Red," he says. "I need to be away from here. And really, it's about fair in my mind since you killed off the guy who owned the place where I worked."

"I didn't kill him, Martin. Alan did."

"I still can't figure out why I'm still here. But I need to go on making a living. There's only one living I know."

"So you'll open a shop much like Andy's? You'll be the new Delphi, then?"

"Yeah, but not here. Somewhere else. Modesto, or Ashlan, maybe. I've got to get away from here. I can't help but to keep going back in my mind over the shooting, over and over again." He shudders and it seems forced.

"Ten-thousand," I say. "That should get you started. Just stay out of our business from now on and we'll be fine. If you ever do see Alan again, I really would consider running for your life."

"Thanks for the heads-up, but I think I'll be fine."

263

"I know what you plan to tell the man when you do see him."

"What's that?" Martin says, playing dumb.

"You're going to tell him about the documents that he's after. You're going to tell him that they exist. Have you discovered where they are?"

Martin looks a little surprised by this. "I've underestimated you, Mr. Scabergrade."

"Have you? Have you found them by searching around in my head?"

"I think so, Red."

"Very well. Do me one favor. Just don't mention the girl. Don't mention Tydomin to him."

He looks over his shoulder at Tydomin sitting in the cab of my truck. "You a little embarrassed because she's too young for you?"

"If that's supposed to be a joke, Martin, it's not funny. Tell him whatever you want about me. Tell him whatever you want about the map. Leave her out of it. This is between you and me and her. We are not like them. That is the only respect I hope to get from you."

"If he asks me, I have to answer."

"He won't. He won't ask you. You'll get your money for the information. And I'm giving you this now to get started. And to get out of our hair. Give me some time to make sure she's safe. Stall him a month or two. You got that? We'll be fine if you can do that."

"We won't be fine. You're forgetting something, Mr. Scabergrade."

"Oh yes," I say. "Thank you, Martin, for showing me my father."

"Thank you, Mr. Scabergrade."

Derek Neely

December 22, 2006

I walk out of Tydomin's apartment a little before I'd like to. I hate leaving things this way; undefined with everyone upset. I can't tell if we've just broken up or if we just had a fight or if she's just out of her mind or what. She's upset, I know that, but I kind of feel like she should be after the lack of respect I feel like I was just shown. When my cell phone rings—a sound I thoroughly despise—I assume that it's Tydomin hoping I'll come back and we can talk things out. I guess that's what I'm hoping, at any rate.

But it's Abigail. I don't really want to talk; I'm kind of talked out tonight. But I also feel bad about the way I left her at the café earlier. Jesus what a capacity for guilt I have. So I press the button and answer.

"What's up Abbie?"

I can hear her sobbing on the other end. "Derek, Derek you have to come over here right away?"

"What's wrong, Abbie?"

"Derek just get over here. You can bring your girlfriend, I don't care just get here as soon as you can."

"Okay, okay, I'm not too far, but I'm on foot, okay? Are you going to be okay for ten or fifteen minutes?"

"I don't know, Derek, just get over here."

Martin Oaks

December 24, 2006

Through Brian's eyes, I can see that the street is
bathed in nothing but fog and Christmas lights strung
high overhead. I follow him as best as I can with so few
people no one besides him around to guide me in
walking down the street. We're trying to be quiet as
we reach the backdoor of the Andante Café.

"It's unlocked, Brian," I say. "I made sure of that
today."

"Does it have to be here? I hate this place."

"It's the safest place for this, Brian. It's our best
bet."

Earlier tonight, Brian came in and he was in pieces.
He had been drinking all day long downstairs at Stones.
Why everyone there continues to serve him is beyond
me. He was broken up about Abigail. About what he
had done to her. I had seen the whole thing playing
over and over in his head when he walked in the door.

They had been in some kind of a fight over the

logistics of their romantic life a couple nights ago. He wasn't even sure what it was about, he's such a dumbass. But she ended up taking him back to her apartment, where he was under the impression that he was going to score. Far from it, Abigail really laid into him about what a poor boyfriend he had been. And before he knew what he was doing, wham, he had hit her. He hit her again and again. Then, as she lay on the ground begging for mercy, he kicked her. Then he stormed out of the apartment.

I asked him if Abbie was okay, and he said that she was. He said that he had checked in on the phone and she said that she was fine. She didn't need a doctor, she was fine.

Brian had initially decided to drop any hopes of a relationship with Abigail after that. But given a couple days to think about the whole thing, he thought better of it. He that that there must be some way to get her back. After all, a little hitting doesn't have to be the end of *everything*. He knew that he could get her forgiveness.

"Don't you think, Delphi? Don't you think that there's some way that she will forgive me? I mean, she didn't file charges, she didn't call the police. She knows that I love her and I know that she loves me. I think we can get passed this."

I wanted to laugh at the thought of this. Then I thought about it a little more deeply. "Brian, there is one measure of devotion that you can show her now. There is one thing that you can do. There is one way that you can elicit a strong enough response from her to get her to reevaluate what she's done to you."

"What she's done to me?"

"That's right, Brian," I told him. "She has misled you. She has broken your trust. She has made you act in a way that you never, ever would have acted without being provoked. She's made you raise your hand against a woman, a sin against God, Brian. This is the way of women, many times, Brian. Deceitful. But we can strike back in ways that she never would have seen, and she will move from the place of pain to the place of passion."

Brian was noticeable cheered by this.

"Tonight, Brian. Tonight we will fix this. In the meantime, don't sober up. You're going to need your courage.

And so that's how at quarter to midnight on Christmas Eve, I find myself breaking into the store room of the Andante Café. Out footfalls make sharp slaps that are muffled by the surrounding moisture. The fog makes everything quiet, nothing reverberates through the fog but the noise dies just as it happens.

We walk into the store room, and everything is dark except for the Christmas lighting coming through the high windows of the store room. I can tell that Brian is reaching groping the walls for a light switch and quickly I stop him.

"Brian," I say. "Don't turn on any lights. We absolutely need not to be caught doing this. Now grab that stool over by the shelves and drag it over here. That's right."

Quietly, Brian picks up a barstool and moves it underneath an exposed rafter. I wander my way over the desk by the door leading to the café. I put down a manila envelope addressed to Abigail Winters. It is an expertly crafted suicide letter in Brian's handwriting.

When I bring my attention back to Brian, I can tell that he is standing on the stool. "I don't know, Delphi. This is extreme. I don't like it."

"No one said it was going to be pretty. You're putting your life in my hands, and I take that very seriously. Don't worry, this will work."

"Go over it again."

"Gently, we're going to set you down. The cleaning crew gets here at twelve sharp, so we don't have much time. They find you, cut you down, and call an ambulance. Abbie gets wind of this, and her heart pours out to you. She won't mistrust you again, she won't push you to extremes again."

He nods and gulps. The rope is tied tightly to the rafter. The noose, which I tied myself, is perfectly crafted to hold Brian's weight. It'd better.

"Okay, now put your neck through the loop."

Again, he thinks twice about this.

"Brian, I told you you'd need to be brave. I told you this is the only way to get your dignity back is by doing this. You don't want to do this, that's fine. You walk away. But you stay away from me and from Abigail after that."

"Just shut up, Delphi, shit. I'm going to do it. Just hold on. Okay." He slips his head through the noose and pulls it tight against his neck.

"Executioners found that there were two ways of going about with hangings, Brian. Those who were most humane would make the rope snap tight, breaking the vertebrae instantly. Death was painless and sudden. But sadistic ones learned that you could hang a man by the neck for hours on end. The neck can stretch a few feet while the person slowly strangles. This second method is what we're going for."

He is sweating and I taking deep breaths.

"Those breaths will help you, Brian; get as much oxygen in your blood as you can right now. But don't worry, settle down. The cleaning crew will be here.

They'll show up and get you down before you've been up there a full minute. The trick is all in the timing. I'm going to let you down slowly, then I'm going to get the hell out of here. I'm going to high tail it out that door and be far away when they come. You're going to be fine, Brian. I have foreseen it."

"Jesus Christ, Delphi, I just don't know," Brian says. "I just can't imagine."

"Stop being such a pussy, Brian," I blurt out. "Quickly, I hear a car. Get ready. Ease yourself down onto your knees and I'll take you down to the end of the rope. There we go. Just relax. There, you're there."

Brian's breathing is quick now that the air flow is cut down, a little lower than I had expected.

"Don't hyperventilate, Brian. You'll pass out. Just relax." Brian does just this and a small little wave of calm passes over him. Then he notices that I haven't left yet.

"Brian, can you hear me?"

He kind of tries to answer.

"It's okay, Brian, I can hear you in my mind. Save your energy and don't over exert yourself. Just breathe. That's it, just breathe." Brian slows his breathing down a little more. He is perfectly still. "Now listen, I want you to hear me and understand me very well. You are a stupid fuck, Brian. You are the dumbest

273

fuck I have ever met in my entire life. Can you hear me? First you go and hit someone much more worthy than you, then you go and believe me when I tell you that the janitors were going to work on Christmas Eve. You're so wrapped up in being a dumb fuck that you actually thought that those two wetbacks were Shinto and didn't celebrate Christmas so they'd come to work. How could you think that, Brian? Just because I told you so?"

There are a thousand questions rushing through his head. The one that makes its way to the fore is *But you told me they'd be here. How could you lie?*

"I did tell you that, Brian, but even if they didn't celebrate Christmas, the janitorial service does. I checked it out. I called Allied Custodial, who Andante gets to clean the floors at night, and everyone is off tonight. You didn't call? What the fuck were you thinking?" I reach out and touch the feet dangling in the air and give them a little push. His eyes are shut tightly, so there's no other way for me to really watch this. "You've lived a bad life, Brian. You're meeting a bad end. You have to see that this is fair."

They'll find me, he thinks. *You'll be caught.*

"Let go of it, Brian. Just stop being so fucking pathetic. They're not coming. The Andante doesn't open until eight o'clock two mornings from now. You'll be a few feet taller, but you'll be dead. No one is going to catch me because this is so clearly a suicide.

"Besides," I say. "No one ever liked you anyway, Brian. It was your need to dominate people that killed you. You're total lack of humility that killed you. Your greed. Your sadistic bullshit attitude to the world that killed you. If you didn't die now, you'd die soon enough. All the people you've hurt, all the lives you've made a negative impact on, you deserve this. You know it."

In the midst of this, he actually has the gall to think of Abigail.

"You shouldn't have hit her, Brian," I say. "You should have walked away when you had the chance. You shouldn't have left that beautiful Caroline girl. She was sweet. And I think you should know now that she never did cheat on you; she never would have done that, not in a million years."

f I could see, I might be able to see the tears running down Brian's cheeks that I can tell he's crying. I sit down on the stool that Brian was standing on and I reach out to play with his feet a little. I think it's a pretty good idea to stay here, stick it out till he's dead, because, as you can imagine, bad shit would go down if he survived this whole thing.

Just like Andy Devidjian a few years earlier, The

Spirit shows me that Brian's candle is burning low, flickering in the wind, and that his life is turning to the smoke.

"Stay with me, Brian," I call out. "I want you to experience every moment of this. If I have to sit here and waste my Christmas Eve watching you die, you'd better be here for it, too."

You fuck! You cock-sucking fuck, Brian calls out in his mind. He tries to open his eyes, but the foggy lights coming in from the window are getting too dim for him to see by.

"Don't talk to me that way, Brian," I say to him. "I'm not the one punishing you. You're punishing yourself here. Now, have you had enough? Are you ready to come down?"

In his mind, Brian's world brightens and he begs, yes he's had enough, yes he's ready to come down.

"I'm sorry, Brian. That was fucked up. I'm just kidding. I'm really sorry about that one." I give his feet a push and he swings back and forth.

Suddenly it's too late for Brian to take place in our rather one-sided conversation. In his mind he is not dangling here from the rafters, but he's an eight year old at his grandfather's house.

It was the last winter that he spent with his grandfather before he died. Brian's mom gave him and his little sister to his grandfather to take care of and never came back. His grandfather was never upset with his daughter for leaving the kids with him; he prided himself on understanding what his daughter was going through. He tried to explain the complications that would bring someone to do something like that in life, but it made no sense to an 8 year-old. He did understand, I could see, loneliness and desperation.

Brian's mind raced. He sees a brown house with wooden shingles covering the roof. There was a golden retriever with dark red fur and a snow-white face, several years past his prime. There is a walnut tree in his grandfather's back yard surrounded by a black iron fence. There are yellow and red leaves covering the ground, crunching under footfalls. A brick path surrounded by gardenias leading to the wooden door.

He's dying, I think. His thoughts are racing and making pictures and flash backs, trying to make sense of why this moment would happen to him. His life is flashing before his eyes.

The door opens with a strong shove against the too-thick beige carpet. The house smells of pipe smoke. The dark wood of the hutch where he had baby pictures and the silver dollars that his grandpa would give him. White walls dimly lit by yellow light. A long hallway lined with family pictures, included the one image he would carry of his mother all his life.

The images bleed together and are imposed on one another until it's very hard for me to keep them apart to continue making sense of them. They mix with the taste of beer, Jack in the Box, his grandfather's barbeque, peppermint gum, Marlboro Reds. He smells campfires and cedar chips. He hears voices and phrases that are so thickly mixed up I can't distinguish them at all. He is dreaming the nightmare waking dreams of an insomniac and trying desperately to hold the image of this room in his head.

"You still with us, Brian?" I can tell that he faintly hears me say this.

Finally, his labored breathing stops. Maybe an hour has passed. I breathe a sigh of relief. I'm somewhat sickened when Brian's flame flutters out entirely, and The Spirit leaves his head and has no where else to go, leaving me alone in the pitch darkness. At the last minute, I decide to try and recover the suicide note. I hadn't thought of it yet, but I don't want the cops busting down Abigail's door with questions. Plus, that might lead them to me. I make it to the desk and find an envelope. I'm pretty sure this is the one I left, but I can't tell in all of this damn darkness. I thrust it in my pocket.

I find my way to the door and crack it open. I feel my way by memory down the street and up into my shop.

Abigail Winters

December 22, 2006

I unlock the door to my apartment and show Brian in. It's not too messy, which is kind of rare for me, but at the same time I feel like it's probably not worth caring how the place looks on account of Brian. "This is the place," I say.

"Nice, how much do you pay a month?"

"Brian," I say. "I really don't want to sit around and make chit-chat with you. Sit down, let's talk."

Brian takes a seat on the small sofa, leaving me a pretty uncomfortable chair to sit in that doubles as a seat from the table. I don't know why I'm sitting here acting surprised that Brian would be so selfish; I should be used to it by now.

"You can sit here," Brian says patting the small space next to him.

"No, Brian. I'm not sitting next to you." He is visibly hurt by this, and that doesn't feel altogether terrible to me. "I really thought that even you would see how nice it's been to be away from me a couple of days. Don't you think that it just didn't work out? Aren't you fine with that?"

"Didn't work out?" He sounds surprised that I was going in that direction. "It hasn't even had a chance, Abigail. What the hell? You don't break up with someone before they've even had a chance to see what the chemistry is like."

"What the hell are you talking about, Brian?"

"We've hardly kissed, Abigail. You're such a prude that your making us wait for some predetermined deadline before you let this thing get physical. I'm just trying to hold out until we've reached your quota of dates so I can prove to you how great things can be between us."

I can't help but to start laughing at this. Somewhere in the back of my head, I decide I'm probably not going back to Delphi for any advice any time soon.

"See what I'm saying, Abbie?"

"No, Brian, I have no clue what you're talking about. It's just funny, is all. What the hell was I thinking?"

"You're doing it right now, these stupid head games. You're sitting here and messing with me and trying to act like you don't know what I'm talking about. You're trying to act like you haven't been dicking me around these last few weeks trying to see how far you can drag me before giving in. Isn't that what you're doing?"

"Brian, what the hell are you talking about? We've been going out on *dates*, Brian. I don't have any kind of quota about when I put out, if that's what you're implying. The truth of the matter is that almost every one of our dates has ended embarrassingly. Either you take me somewhere totally inappropriate, or you get stinking drunk and start thinking you're charming or something."

I read the flinch in the flinch in his eyes that he really does think he's charming when he's drunk. Again I have this urge to laugh. I can't imagine what I was thinking in taking him seriously. All it took was a couple days away from him for me to see what a fool I've been over this whole thing. I really can't blame Brian for being a moron or a dickhead or anything. I can only blame myself for being too blind to see what stupid decisions I've been making.

"It's okay, Brian. I don't blame you. I don't think this is your fault, I'm just realizing. But we can't date anymore. We're through. I don't mind hanging out once in a while, because you're probably a pretty fun guy when nothing's on the line."

"What the hell is that supposed to mean?" Brian stands up, like I've called him out.

"I'm just saying that if I weren't dating you and constantly fending off your trashy suggestions that we get naked, I might think you were pretty fun to be around. You lower your voice, I have neighbors, you know."

"You know? You're full of shit. Why the fuck did you bring me back here, anyway?"

"Why did I bring you here?"

"This is another one of your mind games; another one of your teases. You bring me back here and we both know why. We both know what we're expecting when we go to your apartment, and then you act like you weren't planning to sleep with me at all. You fucking whore."

I stand up now and stand in his face. "You take that back. I would never bring you back here to sleep with you. You wanted to talk somewhere private and I figured it was the least that I could possibly do in breaking up with you. But you can leave now. And I take it back; I don't want to hang out with you. I never want to see your goddamn face again."

Suddenly there's a flash of white and I'm stumbling backwards. I scream and it happens again. Brian hits me with his fists closed three times before

283

my face is pressed against the Oriental rug. Then I feel his foot connect with my ribs. This is it. I'm going to die. I'm going to die. And just as I think that, I see him walking towards the door.

"You fucking whore!" he screams out. "Bitch."

Derek Neely

December 22, 2006

I get to Abigail's apartment and pound on the door. Through the little window in the dining area I see the curtain pushed aside for an instant. Then the door unlocks in three separate clicks.

"Jesus Christ, Abbie." Abbie looks exactly like shit. Her eyes are swollen and there is a trail of dry blood coming out of her nose. "What the fuck happened?" I help Abbie to the couch and have her sit down.

"Will you look at my eyes, Derek? I don't know if I have a concussion or not."

I look at her eyes and they are bloodshot. They both look like they're closing up they're so swollen. "I don't know what I'm looking for Abbie. What the hell happened to you? We have to get you to the emergency room."

"No, no. I really don't want that." As she says this, her arms wrap around her body, like she's shielding herself. I realize that a lot of why she doesn't want to go to a doctor is because of the scars on her body. "I just want you to stay with me, Derek. I just want to talk to you." I hold her against me and let her cry.

285

***

Forgive me, please, this third and final intrusion. I promise it will be the last.

Let's just watch this:

"Vic, we really have to talk."

"What's up, Ty?"

"Walk with me a little, Vic. Just down this way."

They walk down an alley towards the lighted mission.

"Vic, you cannot cancel practice tomorrow night, do you understand me?"

"Why would I cancel practice? We have a big show coming up and we're a bit rusty. Say, how did you get in tonight anyway? Wasn't it an 18 and over night?"

"Vic, promise me you won't cancel practice. You won't get in the car with your little brother."

"Fine, whatever. Isn't it your bedtime?" He laughs, almost eerily. "I'm sorry, Ty, I'm not feeling too good. Something I ate. Or drank, I don't know. Why the hell do you care about practice anyway? Is this something about what Erica said about you? You think you have visions of the future?"

"Erica *knows* I do, Vic. Don't put words in her mouth."

"So what happens if I get in the car with my

brother, anyway?"

"You would die, Vic. I'm worried about you anyway, you know? Does anyone know about this drug problem of yours?"

Vic stops. Vic stares at her, his eyes crimson in the darkness. "Who told you about it?"

"It's kind of obvious."

"Well, fuck off, little girl."

"Whatever, Vic, just don't get in the car."

"Or I'll die, I get it. I'll be a good boy and go to practice."

Tydomin pats Vic on the shoulder and continues walking down the path. He reaches into his pocket and pulls out another cigarette.

And then it hits me. I realize what has just been offered to me: a way out. A clean slate. No ones feelings hurt, no mess for my family to fuss with, no guilt, no blaming, just a nice, clean accident.

"Hey," I call out after the girl. "Hey, Ty!"

She turns around, walks back. "What's wrong, Vic?" Her face sort of contorts up in confusion. "And why the hell are you still getting into that car tomorrow night?"

"Ty, are you *sure* about that? Are you *sure* that I die if I get in the car? And Derek is okay?"

"Derek is fine, Vic, but am I not getting through to

you? You *die*, Vic!"

"But Derek is fine, right? And I die, and it's quick, and there's no suffering?"

"Oh, Jesus Vic, oh no! This isn't right!"

And that's how it happened. That's how it came about. That's how I made up my mind and why she blames herself so much for planting the idea in my head. A clean slate. A way out.

I'd take this moment, if I could, to apologize to her. I'd take this moment, were I still alive, to tell my brother how sorry I am. When it's all said and done, I can't say I made the right decision. But how often is something like that present to someone? A decision to accidentally end your own life. It's extraordinary and terrible. And watching what it put everyone through, it just doesn't seem worth it. I just don't seem worth all the trouble. But the trouble is there, and it's done, and if I could, I would tell them all how goddamn sorry I am for everything I put them through.

I'd also take this moment to tell my brother to forget about me, for Christ's sake; take her already. I know you've liked her a long time, kiss her already. And he'd know exactly who I was talking about, just stop worrying about what I would think.

But dead people aren't really known for their abilities to communicate. I'm stuck watching, reading the pages of this disjointed narrative, the chess movements of my brother and my best friend a mystery to me.

Watching *this* over and over is the worst part:

"Vic, you're making a mistake," Tydomin calls after me.

I walk more lightly back to the bar. The shadow of a smile I have on my face for the first time in a long time isn't a mask I put on for other people to think I'm just fine. It's for my own satisfaction, the way a smile should be.

sol smith

chapter 9

sol smith

Tydomin White

March 16, 2005

I've been living with Erica for about three weeks now. She's a sweet girl, though a bit obtuse and very into her own problems. I have to say that as I saw the events of living with her, I have to say that I was really worried about living with someone who describes herself as a witch. It seemed an awful thing to be proud of. But since living with her, I've discovered that her religion is beautiful and enlightening, even if it's not for me. I don't spend a lot of free time with her, or anything. She rarely asks where I'm going, and I'm fine with that. I'm especially grateful for that tonight.

I drive up to the foothills. There's a small lookout spot that I know of where I've seen cars parked going to and from my old home with Red. I sit on the hood of my car, looking up in the direction of my old house. I know exactly where it is, and I know exactly what I'm here to see. I check my watch.

It's small, very small. Most people would miss it entirely. If you weren't looking for it, you'd never, ever see it. Just a little flare of orange tucked between trees. The house was positioned so that we had a view of the valley below, but it was hidden behind trees so that we weren't noticeable. I watch as the house where I did so much growing up burns to the ground. Just as planned. Just as Red and I had seen. It's much more heartbreaking and painful to watch than I had ever thought. I reasoned that from this distance, and knowing it was going to happen anyway, it wouldn't be a big deal for me to see. I had to watch, though.

But it is. It hurts. Physically, it hurts.

The worst part is that Alan got away. Red didn't. And as far as we can tell, Alan knows that Red is dead and reasons that I am, too. And that Red's work is lost.

It would be a shame for all of Red's work to be lost to the ages. He's done so much in his life, and though there are plenty of ethical concerns with the documents, I just don't see how we could let them go. And that's why we didn't. That's why they're in a safe deposit box tucked away in my name. And that's why Alan had to think that I died in the fire.

I get back into my car and start the engine. I wait for a minute; I look at my watch again. Here he comes.

Racing down the hill going 80 or so, is Alan. His

white Chevy Trailblazer zips down this dangerous stretch of winding road toward Ashlan. I'm guessing that he is fleeing the scene as fast as he can, conspicuous though it seems. He probably figured that Red would have some kind of alarm, some kind of warning, or that the fire would be more visible than it is. So he's running.

Alan isn't through killing for the night. Once inside town, I can see that he will slam into the side of a little Saturn coupe. He will kill the boy riding in the passenger side. As far as I can tell, Alan will get away.

And I know now, for sure, that it's my fault he dies. And it's not because he didn't listen to me, but because he did.

Martin Oaks

December 27, 2006

I walk into the Oak Leaf Bookstore on Olive. It is late
and most of the shoppers returning books they aren't
going to read have come and gone by now. There are a
few people wandering the isles and there is of course
the girl behind the counter. The Spirit keeps one of the
pairs of eyes in my head at all times, so I don't
stumble, so navigation isn't much of an issue.

I'm walking into her den, and I know it. What little
I know about seers comes from the conversations I
would overhear between Andy and Alan. The only
things I learned from those conversations is that a seer
knows when you're coming. You have to act like you
know that they know, like all the cards are out on the
table. This is very different from dealing with a
normally perceptive person. Them, you can play with,
you can manipulate. But, for the most part, a seer has
to be treated like an equal. This is frightening to me.

I approach the counter.

"Hello, Martin," she says. "Hung anyone lately?"

"Please, Tydomin, not so loudly. Do you have a break or anything coming up?"

"Why, Martin. I doubt that we have anything to say to each other."

"Oh, but we do, my dear. Let me buy you a cup of coffee at that place of yours. Oh darn, I saw that the police have that place blocked off today. No problem, let's go to Stone's, what do you say?"

She looks at me inquisitively. It's hard for me to tell exactly what she's thinking since things are so muddled up in her mind. She's looking backwards and forwards with few thoughts about what it is I'm doing right now. It's a maze of thoughts and visions and I just have to wonder how it is she gets herself dressed in the mornings.

I feel around in everyone's heads at Stone's, while waiting for the girl to show up. I listen to the conversations people have with themselves while they look like they're talking to someone else. Men trying to lay women, women trying to out-do each other, self-consciousness. Pathetic worries and concerns worming their ways into their heads.

It's obvious to me when Tydomin comes in because it's like having an entire circus of people flock into the room all at one time. She thinks in so many different ways while managing to keep her feet moving one after the other in a straight line. It's amazing and admirable. Perhaps I am the only person she has ever met who can truly appreciate what a good job her little Daddy Red did of raising her.

Truth be told, I'm happy to see she's alive.

She sits down next to me at the table. "Hi," she says. "Please stay out of my head, Martin. Can you promise me that? Stay out of my head and we can have a conversation. A very productive conversation."

"Now, now. I'm happy to stay out of your head, Tydomin."

"I mean it, Martin. I might sound like I'm being stupid for trusting you, but I seriously, seriously am saying this for your own good. Stay out of my head. If you don't, by the time this conversation is over, you will be in serious pain. No joke, Martin."

I look at her and laugh. I didn't see anything in her mind that alluded to this violent threat coming from a thin teenager.

"I'm serious, Martin. It's for your own good."

"I get the picture, Ty," I say. "No invading personal space."

"Good. Just go somewhere else and watch us or whatever."

I smile at her. I admire her even more now. "Where did you learn so much about how I work?"

"Red wrote pages and pages about telepaths for me to study up on for this conversation. He told me you'd find me sooner or later and that you would still want his precious map. He told me everything I could do to defend myself from the way that you work. But I'm not trying any of them."

"Interesting," I say. "And why not? You obviously know why I'm here. And I'd just like to say that it was a welcome shock to see that you survived the ordeal up on the mountain."

"I wasn't there, Martin. And I choose not to fight you because I'm willing to give you what you want. Do you understand me?"

Again, I can't help but to laugh. I laugh loudly and hope that the other people in the bar don't pay too much attention to us. "Really? You're going to go and turn over this thing that you've worked your whole life to protect? That sounds really likely, Tydomin. Yeah, I'll just stay out of your head for this one and take whatever it is you have in your envelope and go and try and get money for it. You are a clever girl."

"I'm serious, Martin," she says. "I'm going to give it to you, and you can keep it or sell it or destroy it or whatever. But you will tell whoever your contact is or

whoever wants this that I don't have it any more. I
want you to swear by this to anyone who knows about
the cursed thing. And you can have it."

"I could swear that you're serious, Tydomin."

"I am," she says. She lifts a backpack from the
ground next to her feet and throws it on the table. "It's
all there. And the minute I let you walk away with it, I
will be a free woman. Do you understand?"

"What do you think I'll do with it?"

"I imagine you will sell it to that Alan character. A
man who has killed people who you and I care about.
And he will win. And I don't care."

"I never cared about Andy. Don't go assigning
emotions to me."

"Well, whatever. He can have it. And you can tell
him this, if he wants to know: that whole map was
built around a future that was *certain* that the map
would never be discovered. The minute it is acted
upon, the world changes and the rest of the
information will be of no value. You'll have a stack of
CDs that isn't worth anything. And that's the shame of
the whole thing. That this art form will be lost to the
ages. The passive viewing of the future that Red built
his life around will be turned into meaningless drivel.
No evil will come of it."

"Are you certain of that?"

"No. I'm not certain of anything the minute you take this from me. But take it. Take it and just stay away from me."

"And stay out of your head."

"I swear, Martin. You'll regret it otherwise."

I look at Tydomin from the point of view of a woman sitting a few tables away. From what I can gather of her appearance, she's stoic and deadly serious. I reach my hand over and place it on the backpack. I pull it towards myself.

I watch as Tydomin collapses, her head falling into her hands. She lets out a scream which draws a great deal of attention. I stand and put my arm around her.

"It's okay, everyone. Migraines," I say. I walk her out the door as she moans in pain. "You going to be okay?"

"This is why I didn't want you in there. It's painful as hel . But yeah, I'll be fine. Go. Do whatever it is you're going to do."

"Come on upstairs, for Christ's sake."

"No, Martin, no. I don't want anything else to do with you. And I have somewhere I have to go. Just go."

I leave her there, sitting on the ground, her head in her hands.

Derek Neely

December 27, 2006

I ran over to Abigail's apartment as soon as I saw the newspaper headline my dad was reading. I snatched it out of his hands and took it with me. I have a key to Abbie's place now; we reasoned that she might be safer with me having access. So without knocking, I let myself in.

"Jesus, Derek, knock for Christ's sake," she screams, wrapping herself in a towel. She tucks it around herself. On her chest, I can see the scars from her cutting. Of course I can't be sure, but some of them look pretty new. "Will you get the hell out of here for a second?"

"No," I say. "Look at this." I slap the paper down in front of her. The headline on the local page is about Brian. He was found dead the previous morning in the back of the Andante. We read through it together.

"Jesus, Derek," she says. "What do you think happened?"

"They say it was a suicide."

We are quiet for a few moments. I wonder at first what her reaction will be. I'm thrilled, ecstatic, couldn't be more excited. But it occurs to me only the face of her scaring, that perhaps she did have some kind of feelings for him, no matter what he did to her.

"Are you okay?" I ask.

"Yeah, I mean, I'm in a daze."

"How do you feel about it?"

She looks over the article again. I can see tears in her eyes, which have done a tremendous amount of healing in the last couple days. She wipes them away. "I'm happy, Derek. That's how I feel about it. I'm goddamn happy." She bursts into tears and I hold her close to me. She looks up into my eyes and we kiss. We kiss hard and passionately. We find something inside of each other, all of a sudden, that had been growing for a long time. And my concerns about how Vic would see this fall aside.

Tydomin White

December 27, 2006

My head is screaming with pain. It's a thousand times worse than the last time I did something so stupid. It kills me and I hardly feel like I can walk. But I make it down Olive back to my apartment, where Derek is waiting to meet me.

"Derek, I'm sorry I'm late," I say. "Here." I open the door and let him in.

"Did you read about what happened to Abigail's boyfriend?" Derek asks.

"I know, Derek. I'll tell you about that later. I have something I have to say to you."

"Are you okay, Tydomin? I have something to tell you, too."

"Derek, sit down." Despite my screaming head, I'm excited, I'm giddy, I just can't wait to tell him. "I did it. First of all, I sold that painting today. Second of all, I changed things."

"What?"

"I changed things, Derek, I really did. I wasn't

scared, I wasn't cautious, I just took things in my hands and I changed them, and it feels so good. It's a long story, but I shattered the entire future I used to be able to see. I'll be able to see the future again in a couple days, when the pain in my head clears up."

Derek stands up and looks me in the eyes. "Jesus, have you been crying? You do look you have a headache."

"That's an understatement. My whole brain has to reorganize and it is going to ache like hell for days. I just wanted to tell you this. While the headache goes on, at least a week, I'm guessing, I can't see the future. I can't see it at all. I'm lost in the present."

Derek sits back down and brings me down next to him. But he sits at a distance, not touching me.

"So I have the power to make a decision, Derek. For the first time that I can remember, I can make a decision. And I want to choose to give us a chance. I wanted to sell that painting, but I want to give us a chance, too. Let's talk, let's think about what we want, what we can do with our lives, how we want to live them." I'm giddy and excited. I hold Derek's hands in mine.

Derek looks at me with a lost expression on his face; not at all the excitement that I'd hoped to find. There's something on his mind, and it's not me.

"What's wrong, Derek? This is what you've wanted."

"You're right, Tydomin," he says at last. "We've got a lot to talk about, a lot of decisions to be made."

And for the first time, I have no idea what it is he's going to say.

the end

sight